AS KNOWING GOES

A novel by

Valerie Norris

Published by
Llyfrau Cambria Books, Wales, United Kingdom.
*Cambria Books is a division of
Cambria Publishing Ltd.*
Discover our other books at: www.cambriabooks.co.uk

For my husband, Chris Norris. Thank you, Chris,
for your love and support throughout this project and always.

'We know so many things, as knowing goes'

From the volume *As Knowing Goes and Other Poems*
by Christopher Norris, Parlor Press (2022)

About the author

In her professional career, Valerie was a Materials Engineer. She was awarded a Royal Society Research Fellowship that took her to Swansea University where she went on to be awarded a Chair and later became Head of the Materials Research Centre. She took early retirement in 2013. The high point of her career was to be honoured with the title 'Welsh Woman of the Year' in 1998, which led to many activities in public life. In 2004, she was invited to Buckingham Palace as one of the 'Top 180 female achievers in the country'. As well as her novels, she has written and published some 370 research papers and five textbooks in a previous name, Valerie Randle, and has given lectures all over the world. She has achieved an entry in *Who's Who*.

Valerie was born and educated in Kidderminster, England. Wales has been her home since she moved there at the age of eighteen with her first husband. She has been widowed twice and met and married the philosopher-poet Christopher Norris not long after her retirement. She has two children, six grandchildren and three step-grandchildren. Valerie likes to spend her time singing in various acapella groups, long-distance walking, practising yoga and meditation, and writing. For the last twenty years she has volunteered with Cruse Bereavement Support.

Previous novels by Valerie Norris, also published by Cambria Books:

In the Long Run
The April Letters
Beyond Closure
Further Beyond

CONTENTS

Chapter 1

Nothing can beat a May morning in Wales after it's stopped raining and the sun has made its cautious appearance from behind the clouds. Kevin drove his beat-up Ford Escort down the track, avoiding the ruts if he could. The car lurched into their secret place – a gravelly carpark in a woodland clearing.

'Got the picnic?' he said.

Lucy patted her tartan duffel bag. 'Cheese and pickle sandwiches with crisps as usual. And guess what – I've got two bottles of beer! I persuaded our Tom to get it for me last night.' She brandished the bottles of Double Diamond like a pair of dumbbells, large in her petite hands.

'Bet you've forgotten the bottle opener.'

'No, I haven't.' She rummaged in the bottom of the bag and pulled it out, swinging it in front of Kevin's nose.

'I'm impressed. I might have to marry you one day.'

'Oh yeah? Who says I'll say yes?'

Lucy's giggles and shrieks when Kevin pounced and tickled her could be heard outside the car, yet the woodland animals and birds were undisturbed. Eventually the couple tumbled out and went further down the track on foot, Kevin with the duffle bag over his shoulder and Lucy with a rug slung over her arm. Further on the fresh green of the trees gave way to another clearing and the path narrowed and picked up a stream. They spread the rug and tucked into their picnic, half hypnotised by the trickling stream, the timid sunshine, and their love. Their transistor radio was playing a song by David Bowie.

The sun made dappled patterns on their clothes and skin as they lazed replete. 'I will marry you, you know,' said Lucy.

He stroked her hair, marvelling as ever at its blonde abundance. 'I can't see your parents liking that much. Not yet anyway.' He wound a curl around his fingers. 'Maybe we could get engaged. Would you like that?'

She smiled and stretched like a cat on the rug. 'I think I might like that very much. But what will your Mam say?'

'Oh, she'll be OK. And,' he ran his fingers over her cheek, 'she used to say that she'd give the girl I married her diamond engagement ring. It's sort of a family heirloom, and there's some story about how she came by it. And it's worth a bob or two.'

Lucy looked up at this boy she was in love with, taking in his untidy brown hair falling onto his shoulders. 'I don't care about that. Anyway, I might prefer to have my own ring.'

Sometimes you think you've remembered the past just how it was. But you can't be sure.

*

Seven minutes past two. He was late. Carrie pulled her phone out from her shoulder bag. No messages. She scanned the road for sight or sound of a car, but there were several trees, which blocked the view. If he didn't put in an appearance soon, she wouldn't make her three o'clock. She dialled his number, but there was no reply. Hopefully that meant he was on his way, but you never knew. Some people weren't the least bit bothered about letting you down. Carrie buttoned her coat. Even though it was March and there were daffodils nodding under the trees, it was still quite chilly, especially when you were just standing there. She was pushing the last coat button through its hole when a car swept into the drive and pulled up abruptly.

It only took him a minute to extract himself from the driver's seat. Carrie waited, her official estate agent's smile affixed to her mouth and her clipboard clutched against her chest.

'Sorry I'm a bit late,' he said, struggling to get his arms to make their way into his suit jacket. 'The traffic was crazy.' He smoothed his left hand over his already tidy hair. 'I'm Neil Harvey.'

'No problem, I know what it can be like.' She returned his firm handshake and introduced herself as Carrie from Gidson's Property. A hint of an accent; she couldn't quite place it. 'I understand you've come to see our ground floor flat. Shall we?' Carrie started to lead the way, wanting to get started but not to rush him. She had to contain her impatience when he paused to look up at the old house, hands in his pockets.

'It obviously wasn't purpose built as apartments, right? It's been divided up?'

He said 'apartment' and not 'flat'. That, and the two terse sentences gave Carrie all she needed to know: that there was American with some other more familiar twist in his speech. Not that it mattered at all. She just liked to play the game of speculating on origins. He nodded slowly when she told him that there were four separate units in all, and this one had its entrance round the back, which was where she led him. To her surprise he said, 'Nice back yard,' letting his gaze wander over the raggedy grass and unevenly paved patio. She considered it unkempt and thought it let the development down somewhat.

'It's a shared space for all the tenants,' said Carrie as she unlocked the door. The cleaner had been in – you could never be sure – and the flat smelled agreeable. He sauntered behind her, touching walls here and there, opening cupboards in the kitchen, running a tap in the bathroom, throwing questions at her now and again.

'The French doors are neat,' he said. 'Leading out into that garden. Yup, I like that. Are you the sole letting agents for all the apartments? Do you know the other tenants? I'm looking for some peace and quiet, you see.' He turned his interrogating gaze on her. A man not afraid to ask for what he wanted.

He seems quite young to be seeking a quiet life, in his late 40s, she thought, but it wasn't her business to speculate. She was able to tell him promptly that upstairs above this flat was a lady teacher, in the Garden Flat next to him was an elderly lady and on the other wing of the house, taking in both storeys, were a young couple with a child. But you couldn't hear them from this flat. She spoke confidently, sure that would reassure him that there were no students or late-night parties. Her senses pricked up. You didn't go asking about other tenants unless you were interested.

'Could you excuse me while I send a quick message?' she said. 'You carry on having a look round.' Her fingers flew over her phone while she told her three o'clock that unfortunately she had been delayed but she'd be there soon. She had an instinct that it would be worth it not to cut Neil Harvey short, and she wasn't usually wrong in these things.

*

As it happened, no-one saw Neil Harvey move into the ground-floor flat of The Beeches. The removal men were in and out in a jiffy and Neil didn't have much stuff anyway. The furniture and boxes had been hauled out of storage where they had reposed for the last ten years and now stood haphazardly in the three rooms which comprised his new home.

Well, this was it. I might as well make the best of it, he thought. He opened the French doors and strolled out onto the patio. Not a bad garden, but it could do with having its abundance tamed with a little weeding and pruning. Diana would soon have seen to that. Diana. The same bewilderment when he thought of her, the same resolution not to think of her again. It never worked. He wondered what she was doing now. He checked his watch and saw it was nearly midday, so in New York she'd just be getting up, wandering round in her bathrobe, all tousled and appealing. Putting the coffee on to brew. Hot, strong, black and sweet was how she liked it. Just like my men, she used to say. And he had thought she was joking.

Anyway. He went back indoors and pulled open boxes, trying to find the kettle. No luck. But at least he found the mugs and the microwave was already standing on the worktop, so he was able to heat water to make a drink. He lugged his computer out of its packaging and set it up on the desk. So far so good. He gazed at what would be his workstation. Yes, it was a good space. He would be able to work here.

*

Miss Betts, Sarah Betts, noticed the unfamiliar car as soon as she walked into the drive at The Beeches. Well, you couldn't miss it, could you, because there were only usually two cars here, and neither of them was hers. She had to take the bus every day into town. That was less than a mile but then she had to get another bus out in another direction to her school. A little car was her dream, rather than struggling with books and sharing space with all those people on the bus.

The entrance to her flat was at the back, the same as the new tenant's. She let herself in through the door to the small hallway from which the stairs led off to her upstairs entrance. She paused and stopped shuffling her bags, straining to hear any noises that might be coming from the tenant in the downstairs flat, but all was silent. Ah, well. No doubt their paths would cross sooner or later.

*

It worked perfectly for Lucy to have Alice's once-a-week video call on a Friday evening, making a welcome change from television or reading. Although Lucy did get out to the theatre, dining or to see friends quite often, those activities tended to drop off during the winter months. But now the clocks had changed to British Summer Time, and you could really notice the extra daylight in the evenings. The Garden Flat, with its ample windows, let in lots of light and gave a feeling of being a part of the outside world while still being cosy indoors. It was the first thing that had attracted her to the flat.

'G'day Mum! How are you doing?' Alice, hair all tousled from bed, was in her pyjamas. Pretty pink affairs with short, puffed sleeves, they were. Just what you might expect her to wear first thing of an early autumn morning out there in Sydney. She sat in her spacious lounge, with various houseplants and framed photos clearly visible in the background.

'I'm good, thanks.' It was Lucy's standard response. The last thing she wanted to do was to let on to Alice how various aches and pains intruded increasingly, and a visit to the doctor last week resulted in an increased dose in her prescription of blood pressure tablets. Alice would do her loving best to orchestrate care for her mother from the other side of the world, which was a nice way of saying she would fuss. 'And how are you, love? How's your nasty cold?'

'It's getting better now, thanks. I'm drinking plenty of vitamin C.' Alice brandished her glass of orange juice and took a glug. They both knew how to play the game of glossing over the truth so as not to cause worry.

'Ah, good. A bad cold can make you feel awful. How's the weather out there?' Another stock topic that had to be got out of the way.

'Same old same old. I thought today I could hit the beach with the kids for a barbie, to get the last of the summer. Wish you were coming with us, Mum.' By way of explanation for Zoe and Joe being with her, Alice added, 'They're both home for the weekend because it's their dad's birthday tomorrow and he's having some sort of bash, I gather. They're staying with me because I've got more space.'

Lucy could picture Alice with Zoe and Joe loading up the car and heading out to the coast. It was nice that her teenage grandchildren still wanted to go out with their mum sometimes. She had to get her head around the fact that they were nineteen and eighteen and lived in Halls at university now. By all accounts – that is, what Alice said, rather than what they told her – they had both settled into university life well and were having fun. Lucy did wonder if having fun was the primary reason for being at university, but she thought better than to question. It still smote her that she hadn't seen than much of Zoe and Joe while they were growing up. There had only been one or perhaps two trips per year, although she did keep in touch as best she could via photos, letters and phone calls, and latterly email then messages. And now suddenly they had metamorphosised into fully-fledged adults. Well, she wasn't sure about the fully-fledged bit, but they were certainly adult sized. Last time Lucy had visited, when Kevin was still alive, Joe had towered over his grandad.

Memories of last year's trips to the beach with the family and fun afternoons of sun, sand and laughter flickered in Lucy's head. 'Hopefully we'll all go to the beach at Christmas,' she said (note to self: get on the case about booking an air ticket).

It was so precious to have this dedicated one-on-one time with her daughter, even though she was ten thousand miles away. Hurray for Zoom and WhatsApp, which had been virtually unheard of before the pandemic. Certainly not a 'thing' back then. Easily, she settled into gossiping with Alice just as if they were both sitting on her sofa, sipping tea and eating Alice's favourite custard cream biscuits. She relaxed so much that she nearly forgot her main news of the week. 'Oh, by the way, I've got a new neighbour. Remember I said the flat next door had been let? Well, he's moved in now.' Alice, gratifyingly, asked for details.

It had been a few days since the new neighbour had first appeared. Lucy had spotted him because you had to go past her door on the side of The Beeches to get to the other two flats and the garden at the back. That was apart from Jane and Lesley's flat, which was accessed from the front door. There was a trellis between her Garden Flat and the path, which worked well to preserve just enough privacy. Then yesterday she had encountered him properly while he was unloading Tesco's bags from the back of his car. It only took one appraising look to ascertain that he was tall, good looking and quite young. Well, anyone who was fifty or younger counted as 'quite young' to Lucy nowadays.

The conventional, not-too-nosy question to ask was 'how are you settling in?' and she had asked it.

He smiled as he answered. A pleasant, open smile. 'Great. I'm very happy with the place. No problems. The Wi-Fi is up and running, so I can start working.'

She didn't miss the accent, but it was too soon to make enquires. 'Anything I can help you with, just knock on my door.'

'That's kind. I'm new in town, so I might take you up on that.' He held out his hand. 'I'm Neil'.

'Nice to meet you, Neil. I'm Lucy'.

Chapter 2

People sometimes wondered why Lucy Jones had chosen to move to The Beeches rather than to a dedicated retirement home. Such a place would be tailored to the needs of an elderly person and the exclusive company of other people in your own demographic. In particular Alice was very much in favour of such a move. 'Mum, a retirement home sounds just perfect,' she had said. 'You haven't got to be responsible for the garden or anything, and think of all the new friends you'll make. And it would give me peace of mind to know you have some backup.' Lucy had sought to reassure her, while quashing down her guilt because she could understand her daughter's point of view. 'I wish you weren't so far away, Mum.' Alice had placed her fingers on the screen so that Lucy could press her own against their image. Never very satisfactory, she thought. For her it only emphasised the absence of physical contact between them, rather than assuaged it.

It was when Lucy had passed the milestone of three-score-and-ten years that she had realised she should think about the future. Her future, without close family in easy reach. The decision to move out of her three-bedroomed house, where she had lived for more than thirty years and seek a more fitting home was brought forward by two things. The first was a simple accident, a slip where she broke her wrist and bashed her face. It could have been worse, she told herself, but her confidence and joy in her independence had been knocked. And, of course, then there was lockdown, which had knocked everybody's confidence.

And so the quest to find a new home became real instead of a vague intention for the future. A sheltered housing complex, designed for the over 60s, was the obvious choice and there were several about. A couple of her friends lived in one such place near town, so she had a fair idea of what life would be like there – communal laundry room where someone accidently walked off with your washing instead of their own, chair yoga in the shared lounge, leaning on your walking stick while you gossiped in the corridors. There were good points too, which her friends earnestly assured her swung the balance: the administration of the house manager, the emergency pull cords in all your rooms, the cleaning and maintenance of everything outside your own flat taken care of via the hefty service charge that you paid in advance every year. Plus, right outside the one where her friends lived were a Co-op and a Post Office, and buses to the centre.

Lucy was wary of living in such proximity to friends, much as she liked them socially. Then she saw an advert for Weston Court. Now this wasn't just a retirement complex – it was a retirement *village*. Weston Court was several miles out of town, set in acres of its own landscaped gardens. It comprised a range of luxury flats 'to satisfy the discerning purchaser', a restaurant, a shop, a hairdresser, and a nursing home on-site for when the time came that you needed a little more care. Weston Court had everything the mature person needed for a full life, in fact, including a daily minibus into town if you chose to venture out.

After some weeks of procrastination, Lucy drove out to see the bespoke Weston Court for herself.

'Welcome to Weston Court Assisted Living,' the middle-aged, well-groomed staff member had said to her when Lucy had turned up to see for herself. The woman knew her sales pitch alright: as she guided Lucy around the village, she smoothly expounded the enriched lifestyle waiting for her to experience when she moved to Weston Court.

Yes, it was all so well-appointed, and Lucy was not short of funds, especially once her house was sold, so a one-bedroomed flat in Weston Court was well within her price range. Only one thing was missing: youth. No teenagers with their skateboards and mobile phones, no children playing games, no babies crying, no young professionals cruising into the carpark in their flashy cars. Wherever you looked there was only aged people shuffling doggedly with walking frames, except for the odd scurrying care worker or cleaner. Lucy hated it. She recoiled. Society was not supposed to be like this, with elders conveniently hidden away behind immaculate manicured gardens.

*

The first thing Lucy did after she had parked the car on her drive and let herself into her house where she had lived for the last few decades was to wash her hands thoroughly, and splash water on her face as an afterthought. It certainly wasn't that Weston Court was dirty, quite the opposite. It gleamed, sterile and orderly. She just wanted to rid her body and mind of the fake floral smell and taint of the place. After patting her face dry she examined herself in the mirror. Her silver-grey hair was neatly cut to jaw length, and her skin housed a tracery of wrinkles, yet her eyes gazed back, as intelligent and keen as they always had been. Why was there an old lady living in her mirror?

She hung the towel back on the rail and went into the bedroom where her little collection of framed photographs was housed. She picked one up and felt the dust under her fingers. That just showed how often she cleaned and, more to the point, how often she picked these pictures up and really looked at them.

'I'm not old, am I, love?' she murmured to the smiling face in the picture. It had been taken on a holiday in Italy a few years ago, before Kevin got ill. He was beaming in the sunshine, unaware of the disease that had already started to nibble inside his body. 'What you, old? You're still only middle aged! Look at all you do, going to the gym, working at the charity shop, still going for walks like we used to – remember?' Yes, she remembered. She could imagine his words, which was the next best thing to hearing them.

No, she could cross Weston Court off her list of potential new homes. She put the picture back on the shelf and went to put the kettle on.

*

'I get it that you didn't want to live in the seniors' village,' Neil had said. 'So why choose this place instead?'

Lucy had given a very expurgated version of her Weston Court experience to Neil when they sat having afternoon tea in her flat. This was the second time they had met like this, and they were both still very much finding out about their respective new neighbour. When she had bumped into him on the drive and offered him a friendly invitation to her flat for coffee to welcome him to The Beeches she had been surprised when he said yes, let alone that he had come for a second time.

The delicacies that comprised Lucy's English afternoon tea reposed between them on her coffee table. Although, it wasn't completely English. Although she had made the traditional little triangular egg and cress sandwiches with their crusts cut off, and scones with butter and jam, she couldn't resist making Welsh cakes instead of something like sponge cake to complete the trio of delicacies. She had dragged her old bakestone out from the back of the cupboard and indulged in nostalgic thoughts of her childhood while she heated it up then watched the dollops of curranty, spicy mixture metamorphosise into something edible. A convenient cross between a cake and a biscuit is the Welsh cake. She could remember her mother standing at the stove expertly flipping the part-cooked Welsh cakes on this very bakestone. And maybe her mother before that.

Neil sat back on the sofa, engaging enthusiastically with Lucy's afternoon tea. A light sprinkle of crumbs dusted his sweatshirt, but then, what man ever used a tea plate to any great effect?

'Why did I choose The Beeches? Well, I was looking for a mix of people (although you can't know for sure how that may change), preferably a ground floor, quite close to town, with access to a garden.' She ticked the list off on her fingers. 'I was starting to lose heart because most of the places I saw online when I looked for one-bedroomed flats were in blocks and had no garden. Then, I saw this place, and it seemed too good to be true. I had a look round, with a

11

nice woman from the estate agent's called… now, what was it…
Carla, or something?'

'Carrie. Yeah, I had her to show me round too. She did a great
job. Wow, she must have been working with them a while. Didn't
you tell me you came here in 2020?'

'Yes, that's right. It's generally Carrie who comes round in the
first instance if anything needs seeing to. Anyway, I made my mind
up to take the flat within half an hour of setting foot in it. I haven't
looked back since. I simply love it here. And all the other residents
are all nice, which is a great bonus. More tea?'

Neil nodded and proffered his cup. He didn't like to tell her that
coffee was really his drink, after all those years in the USA. He knew
he should be getting back to work, but it was kind of cosy here, and
there was great food, that he didn't have to prepare, constantly
coming his way. What was not to like? Tomorrow morning at the
gym he'd work extra hard. And it was a slog getting his own business
off the ground alongside his day job so that he was glad to take a
couple of hours off.

Lucy observed him over the rim of her cup as she sipped her tea.
A good looking, slim man in his late forties, at a guess. Dark hair,
curling down onto his collar, with the first signs of grey. Why is it
that women panic about those incipient greys, whereas on men they
just look distinguished? She had done her share of agonising in front
of the mirror, back in the day, followed by some years of regular
trips to the hairdressers to get her roots done. Then in latter years,
particularly after she retired, she couldn't be bothered with the whole
rigmarole of sitting for ages with her scalp plastered in goo. What
freedom there was in the statement of grey hair.

Lucy appreciated the fact that he hadn't got dressed up to come
to tea. Jeans and flip flops were fine. She hadn't wanted it to be an
occasion, just a neighbourly thing to do. He was a bit of an enigma,
to be honest, and she was impressed but a bit bewildered that he
would want to spend time with an elderly lady. He had told her he
had returned home after ten years in the States and had landed a job
as an accountant, working mainly from home. She had an inkling
that there might be a 'sad tale waiting to unfold,' as her mother

would have said, but she knew better than to pry. Perhaps he'd reveal a bit more as time went on. And she totally acknowledged that she was being blatantly nosy. Or could you describe it as just being interested in people?

*

The garden could definitely do with a bench, thought Lucy as she stood at the sink washing up the tea things. She thought this every time she looked out from her kitchen. She had mentioned it once or twice to Carrie, who had promised to mention it to the office. Nothing ever came of it though, and the residents still had to haul their own garden chairs onto the patio. Mostly the residents borrowed one of Lucy's from her stack by her back door. Perhaps they thought that they were communal.

There was a particularly magnificent lilac tree in the garden which came into bloom at this time of the year. It was starting to go past its best now. A variety of other trees and shrubs fringed the patio, which was the focal point of the garden. Vegetation sprang insistently between the paving slabs, and the flower beds had their share of weeds too. No doubt Frank, who did the garden, would soon be making some visits to coax it back into some sort of order so that nature didn't win completely. Lucy was always a little sad after Frank had hacked and pruned, but she recognised that you needed to keep nature it in control – with a light touch.

During lockdown, when not more than six people had been allowed to meet outside, Lucy had instigated the 'garden meet-ups' of The Beeches residents. At that time a couple of students were living in the flat where Neil had now moved in. So, the two students, Sarah Betts, Lesley, Jane and Lucy had comprised the statutory maximum six who sat in a circle on the patio a few feet away from each other, eating Lucy's cake and drinking her coffee. Although, to be fair, sometimes another resident would chip in with a packet of biscuits or a carton of milk. Lucy thought back over those strange times as she washed the cups after Neil had gone. Their little assembly had bonded in a rather awkward way; they were thrown

13

together by circumstances and propinquity, so quite a bit of the conversation revolved around the government's handling of the pandemic and life in The Beeches. But the other thing that provided the glue for their group was Charlie, Lesley and Jane's baby, who lay in his buggy and sometimes woke up so that one of his two mummies could lift him out to sit on their knee and gaze big-eyed at the ring of smiling people. Lucy had yearned to cuddle the little plump body but, of course, that would not have been allowed in the pandemic-ridden times that they were living through. And now, Charlie was a sturdy little boy of five who skipped around the patio and raced his cars there and knocked on Lucy's door for a biscuit whenever his mummies allowed. Lucy admired Lesley and Jane for having the courage to live their lives in a way that suited them.

That was the washing up all done. It had been nice entertaining Neil, and she hoped he'd come again, although she would leave it a few weeks before asking him. Clearly, he'd got his work cut out settling into his new life. She dried her hands on the towel and picked up her engagement ring from the little dish on the windowsill, put there especially for the purpose of holding it while her hands were in water. She saw the row of five stones gleam as she pushed the ring onto her finger above her wedding band. Does hot water damage the glue and the claw setting for the stones? After all these years she still didn't really know.

Chapter 3

As it happened, it was a very short engagement.

'Are you sure?' Kevin had said while they were snuggled up on the back seat of the Ford Escort, the lay-by dark and sinister outside the car windows.

'I'm three weeks late now, and I've started to feel sick in the morning. That means it's pretty definite. Lucy shivered in the cold and pulled the blanket up further. The same blanket that they had picnicked on back in the summer.

She felt rather than heard Kevin sigh. His face was turned away from her. 'I suppose we'd better get married then. And we can live with my folks until I get my transfer. Perhaps we'll be able to get a council house then.'

Lucy could just make out the looming shape of trees outside. Usually, she was too taken up with their frantic back seat lovemaking to notice anything like trees. But this evening Kevin hadn't even kissed her. 'It'll be fine,' she said. 'I don't mind having a small wedding, and we won't be long living with your parents. After that we'll have our very own home. It will all be OK.' She put all the conviction she could muster into her voice, quelling the panic that was rising inside her. Despite all her manufactured positivity, Kevin remained sunk in gloom. She burrowed her hand under the blanket and undid the zip on his jeans. Soon they had temporarily forgotten the challenges that lay ahead.

How young they were, how naïve.

*

The late spring morning was showing every sign of developing into a decent day as Neil set off from The Beeches in his running kit. Being a Sunday, there was hardly any traffic around and the occasional sound of birdsong was better than the drone of car engines any day. The start of his run was a bit later than he'd hoped. It had taken him two strong cups of coffee to get going because last night he had arranged to meet with an old buddy from years back, before he had moved to New York, and boy, had they caught up. They finished the evening, as was traditional in the UK, with a late-night curry. Neil had forgotten how much stronger British beer was than the American equivalent.

As he was leaving that morning, he had bumped into the teacher lady as he came out to empty some trash. After a quick nod she had scurried back up into her flat, probably because she was still in her robe, which she had clutched round her neck when she saw him. Neil had previously tried to engage her in conversation a couple of times, but she only answered in monosyllables, looking like a frightened rabbit, so he hadn't persevered. Perhaps she had thought he was hitting on her. How old would she be? Hard to tell with those repressed types. She could be anywhere between thirty-five and fifty. Well, perhaps she was just shy. And she wasn't unattractive, really. Especially this morning when her hair was loose and tangled and she didn't have her glasses on.

It was different with the girls who live in the front flat. What were their names? Lesley and Janet? No, Lesley and Jane, that was it. And that cute little boy, Charlie – he was the best. The girls were always smiling and neighbourly when he saw them. Lucy said that it was actually Jane who was Charlie's biological mom, and she had a feeling that there had been a deal done with some guy to be Charlie's dad in the regular way, rather than all that artificial insemination crap. Although Neil had no problem with lesbians, taking in Jane's curvy body where her tight tee shirt clung and showed her prominent mommy nipples gave him the slightly unworthy thought that she was wasted on women.

He was approaching the riverside walkway with its meander of willow trees and benches. The odd take-out container was left on them from last night. The caffeine had kicked in now, and he was powering along easily. His mind slid ahead to the rest of his day. He would probably make a start on that new audit this afternoon. An advantage of his job as an accountant working mainly from home was that he had relative freedom with his time schedule. He was released from the nine-to-five prison sentence. So what if he worked on a Sunday afternoon or at midnight? Of course, this afternoon he could always put some more time into researching the launch of his own online business, but it needed a final push to commit to that.

There were more runners, dogwalkers and strollers now that he was alongside the river, since he was a little late getting started. The whole day was stretching and hitting its stride. It slowed his pace down a little to have to weave around some of these folks and, especially, their dogs. Many of them had earbuds, which plugged them into their own electronic world. So probably they couldn't hear him coming, especially if their eyes were on their screens too. All this disruption of his pace was a little irritating, especially since he'd opted to leave his own portable sound system at home today. He didn't need noise of any kind prodding his hangover.

Perhaps it was best to decide not to treat this run as serious training but more as leisure exercise. So he could just let his mind wander over the set-up he was establishing for his life. He mentally ticked off the boxes. The apartment was good and in a great location, his new job seemed to be working out, and he had launched a social life for himself. Yep, you could say he'd certainly fallen on his feet since he'd been back. Yesterday he had looked out his window and seen Carrie in the garden with a middle-aged guy in boots who Carrie had introduced as Frank who came to keep the garden tidy and do odd jobs. After he had gone out to say hi – well, it was only polite, right? – Carrie had seemed pleased to see him. In fact, he couldn't be sure she wasn't giving him the come-on. There had been that sassy smile and the way she kept touching her hair while she asked him how it was going. He didn't want to take it any further; it might be a bit awkward. But it was good to know he'd still got it if he wanted to get back in the game. *When* he wanted to get back in the game.

And the elderly lady, Lucy, now she really was a sweetie. He felt he could relax in her company. He was reaching the end of the city park with its garishly painted kids' playground, which was his turn-around point, when it dawned on him. Lucy reminded him of his mom in her later years, before she got sick. Something about her openness and interest in what went on around her. And she sure had her finger on the pulse of life at The Beeches – a matriarch, kind of, with her organising them into a little tribe and looking out for them and everything. She seemed to tread the line between being inquisitive and being friendly, and you never felt she was unduly gossipy or salacious. For instance, he had intimated to her that there had been a bad break-up in his recent past, but Lucy had been sensitive enough not to push for details. Would Diana be just waking up now in New York and getting ready to go for a run, like they used to do together? He realised that this was the first time he'd thought about her all morning.

*

'I could tell them on my own, you know. You don't really have to come,' said Kevin, as he and Lucy walked down the road holding hands, the street lamps shedding pools of insipid light onto the pavement.

'Of course I'm coming,' said Lucy, although the reason she was trembling slightly wasn't just the cold evening. 'After all, you came with me to tell my parents.'

'To be fair, they took it very well.'

'I think they were just pleased that you're going to make an honest woman of me, and sooner rather than later is OK. And, of course, Mum is delighted she's going to be a grandmother. She's probably started on knitting bootees already.'

'I still reckon they think you're marrying beneath you. After all, look at your Tom. He's courting quite a wealthy bird, so you've said. Drives her own car and all.'

Lucy squeezed his cold hand. 'Rubbish. Just because you work underground doesn't mean to say you're not every bit as good as the next man. And they know that you love me and I love you.'

'I'm a lucky bloke to have you.' He quickly bent down and kissed her. 'Well, here goes.' They had reached the shabby back door of Kevin's house, and they went in. He took Lucy's coat and scarf from her and hung it under the stairs on a peg.

'Is that you, Kev?' Lucy heard the high voice coming from the next room. They went through, Kevin leading the way and Lucy following. 'Hello, Mam. Look who's here.'

Kevin's mother was sitting in an armchair next to the fireplace, where burning coals were glowing. 'Lucy!' she said. 'This is a nice surprise.' She held out her arms to Lucy, and Lucy hugged her quickly, holding her breath to minimise the tobacco smells. To be fair, Nerys had always been welcoming to her, and Lucy tried to see past the garish make-up and dyed hair.

'Hello, Nerys,' she said. 'How are you?'

'Oh, I'm keeping well, thank you. Sit you down, love. Kev, get two more cups and saucers, will you. There's still some tea in the pot.'

Lucy sat down somewhat cautiously on the settee, which was in front of a magnificent oak Welsh dresser and was the only thing that Lucy liked in the room, if she was honest. The dresser featured glass-fronted doors which revealed a range of crockery on display within. Although, the effect was rather spoiled by the piles of junk on the top of the lower part of the dresser.

They all sat and drank their tea while Kevin and his mother talked desultorily. Lucy mainly smiled and nodded, trying to ignore the smoke from Nerys's cigarette. Kevin's dad was, apparently, in the pub. Kevin drained his cup and put it down decisively on the floor. 'We've got something to tell you, Mam. You see, it's like this. You know Lucy and me have been going out for a while now, and we are serious…'

'Let me guess – you're getting engaged! Is that it?' Nerys looked eagerly from one to the other.

'Well yes, we are, but that's not quite all.' Kevin put his arm round Lucy and drew her to him.

Nerys looked shrewdly at Lucy. 'In the family way, are you girl?' Lucy stuttered out a reply, almost inaudibly. Nerys breathed in sharply and threw her cigarette butt into the fire. 'I knew it. As soon as you walked into the room, I felt it. I can often sense these things, you know. How far along are you? Couple of months or so?'

Lucy confirmed that was the case. 'So, a very short engagement then get on with the wedding, is it?' Lucy couldn't quite get her head around how pragmatic Nerys was being about their news. The three of them talked around the practicalities; how Lucy's health was, where they would live, and other things. Nerys said that she would handle Kevin's dad and that he would do what she told him. Lucy's head was reeling. Her own parents had reacted rather differently. Although they had ended up accepting the news – there wasn't a lot of choice, really – they were clearly shocked and disappointed. But her own home life and Kevin's were different. Basically, she lived in a rather sedate cul-de-sac and Kevin lived on a council estate. Not that it matters, she told herself.

Nerys asked Lucy to bring a stool and come to sit by her. She held Lucy's hand and musingly turned the palm over. 'Lucy,' she said. 'Lucy… that name means 'light'. Did you know that? There was a Saint Lucy back many years ago. Patron saint of the blind, she was. If I'd had a daughter, it's a name I would have liked for her. But instead, I was blessed with two boys.' She glanced up at Kevin, who smiled at his mother, evidently pleased that the big announcement had gone so well.

'You know, Lucy, as soon as I met you with our Kevin, I hoped that you'd be the one. I'm so pleased you're getting married, even if it will be a bit of a rush.'

Lucy felt herself softening towards her future mother-in-law. 'I'll do everything I can to make him happy. I promise.'

This declaration, and Kevin joining in with a similar promise, produced another round of hugs for the three of them. 'Now,' said Nerys, 'I've got something to give you, Lucy.' She held out her hand and drew her engagement ring off her finger and held the ring out to Lucy. Lucy tried not to notice her chipped nail polish.

Lucy was perplexed. 'I can't... I can't possibly accept this! It's yours!'

'Ah, but it's a tradition in the Jones family. The story handed down is that my grandfather stole it from a gypsy to give to his sweetheart, who was my grandmother. Then she gave it to my mother when she married, and she gave it to me. Isn't that right, Kev?'

Kevin shrugged. 'If you say so.'

Nerys gave her son a disapproving look and continued to address herself to Lucy. 'Well, it's all true. And now it's right and proper that it should be yours. Let's do it properly. Come on Kev, put it on her finger.' Kevin obediently slid the ring onto Lucy's left hand. 'Oh look, it fits perfectly! And look how the diamonds are catching the light!'

Lucy sat back down on the sofa with Kevin and responded as best she could to Nerys's excited chat. Surreptitiously, she ran her thumb around the alien presence on her finger and glanced down at the row of five stones that were staring challengingly at her, daring her to refuse the gift. But she knew she couldn't. She would have to bow to Jones family tradition, and no doubt she'd get used to the ring.

Nerys was an enigma to Lucy. She was partly repelled by Nerys's slovenliness, but also a part of her was reluctantly fascinated by the slightly witchy, gypsyish charisma and folklore wisdom. Of course she had said none of this to Kevin. What did this silly ring and its story matter compared to the fact that she and Kevin loved each other and were going to be together and have a baby? She just wished that Nerys had given them the lovely old Welsh dresser instead of the ring.

*

Neil thought he was just getting the hang of his new life back home when *bam*! there it was. During a midmorning break from work he had been idly scanning through Facebook, as you do, and suddenly Diana was staring out of his desktop computer at him. A breeze was allowing her hair to flow softly around her face and there was that lazy, teasing smile, slightly asymmetrical, that he had tried so hard to forget. He could have coped with seeing her image, but she was not alone. Her new man had his arm around her, and his grinning face was close to hers. There was an idyllic view of pristine sands and a turquoise sea behind them where they sat in the sunshine. Her skin looked even fairer than ever against the darkness of his.

When he could tear his eyes away from the taunting picture, he read the caption which informed him that they were vacationing on a cruise around the Caribbean. That was exactly the sort of trip Diana used to try to interest him in, but he didn't feel he could easily afford it. He was comfortably enough off – he could always make his rent, that sort of thing, - but he didn't have the money to splash around on luxury vacations. And to be honest, a cruise wasn't really his thing. Diana could lie happily in sun for hours, slathered in sun cream, while he preferred to punctuate his sunbathing with activities such as running or biking. On board a ship there was no opportunity for either.

Neil snapped off the computer and flung himself out through the French doors into the garden. Well, looks like she's got what she wanted, he thought as he strode onto the patio. The first shock was wearing off and reducing to the dull ache that he had felt in first few weeks after Diana left. Although he did know she had become infatuated with someone else who was wealthier than he was, he hadn't wanted his nose rubbed in it.

The sound of footsteps behind him made him turn around. It was the handyman, whose name he couldn't remember.

'Alright, mate?' said Frank. He was carrying a hedge trimmer.

'Not bad, thanks. How are you?' Neil's polite reply was automatic.

'Mustn't grumble. You're quite new here, aren't you? In the flat next to Lucy's?' Neil confirmed that was the case. 'Nice old girl, Lucy. She usually brings me a cup of tea when she sees me.' He glanced back over his shoulder hopefully. 'She might be out.'

If that was a hint, Neil chose not to take it. 'Well, I won't keep you from your work,' he said. 'And I've got to get back to mine.' He started to edge towards his French doors which he had left open.

'I expect you're going to this shindig tomorrow, then?' said Frank.

Neil frowned, thrown for a minute by the image conjured of cowboys dancing with barmaids. Then he realised that the 'shindig' was the garden party he'd been invited to by Lucy. 'Oh, you mean Lucy's gathering? Gee, I didn't think it was going to be wild! I was only expecting a mixer with some food and drink.'

Frank grunted. 'I don't know because I haven't been to one before, have I? I'm buggered if I know why I've been invited now. Carrie says it's alright to come along if I've been invited, so I suppose it is. She's my niece, you know.'

'Ah, yeah, I'd forgotten that. I think it's really great of Lucy to host us all like this.' Frank still looked grumpy. Neil made an effort and tried to jolly him along. 'You'll have another guy to talk to with me there. C'mon, it'll be great. The weather looks like it's going to be fine.'

'I suppose,' said Frank, picking up his hedge trimmer. 'Well, this garden won't tidy itself. I'd better get on.'

Neil went back into his flat and flicked the kettle on. He went to the bathroom and looked at his face in the mirror, running his hand over the dark stubble on his chin. Naturally he'd shave before he went out tonight to meet his friend. Pull yourself together, man, he said to himself silently. He lifted his chin and stood up straighter. Your life, your new life, is nicely on track. You have a job, the possibility of a bit more earning on the side, somewhere nice to live, you're fit, and you're going to this garden party tomorrow. Plus, you felt a definite flicker of interest when the handyman guy mentioned Carrie. Fuck off, Diana and your new man. I'm doing OK.

*

It had been a surprise for Lucy to see that Alice was up and dressed quite early on a Saturday morning. This time it was Lucy who was in her pyjamas, after having decided to indulge in an early evening bath.

'You're looking nice,' said Lucy. 'Are you off out somewhere?'

'Just a walk, you know.' Alice was sitting at her breakfast table, coffee cup half empty, winter sunshine peeping in behind her. 'Zoe and Joe are here again this weekend, as it happens, but they're still in bed of course. Teenagers, huh? I said to them, it would be nice if you spoke to your grandmother now and again.'

Was it an on-screen thing, or a mother thing, or both, that Lucy could pick up on subtle inflexions in Alice's voice and manner? 'Don't worry about the kids,' she said, 'I message them now and again and they usually reply, so I know they're alive. But this walk of yours… dressed quite smart, aren't you?' Alice was wearing a light jacket over her top, accessorised with an artfully tied scarf around her throat, which picked up the blue of the jacket. Her earrings were gold hoops.

Alice shifted in her seat and rearranged her scarf. 'I didn't say it's going to be a bushwalk, and I don't want to look unkempt, do I?'

It was dawning on Lucy. 'Are you meeting someone?' She thought from Alice's scowl she was going to be told to mind her own business, but Alice admitted that she would be having a companion.

Was it a date? Maybe. Judging from her reticence, Lucy hoped so. Alice deserved some fun after her messy divorce and years of bringing two kids up on her own. She decided that she would probably get more out of Alice by backing off and changing the subject.

'Well, I've got something in my diary for today.' When Alice duly asked her what it was, Lucy told her that she was hosting one of her 'bring a plate' socials for her neighbours. 'The weather is set fair, which is just as well because it's in the garden. It would be a bit of a squash in my flat, especially since Carrie and Frank said they would probably look in too. If you remember, Carrie's the woman who represents the estate agent's that we rent from. She seems to go the extra mile in overseeing us, which is nice. Frank's the gardener and odd job man, and Carrie's uncle, as it happens.' Lucy sometimes had to remind herself that Alice had never actually been to her flat, although she had done a thorough Zoom walk-through in the early days, and there were plenty of images on WhatsApp. Alice had given her somewhat guarded approval. Her preferred choice would still have been for Lucy to go to a retirement complex and get looked after, even though Lucy had steadfastly put forward her reasons for not doing that.

'Why is it always you doing the hosting and organising? Can't you share it around with the others? It seems like a lot of work for you to do.' Lucy controlled her mild irritation at Alice's comments and said, 'The others all have full-time jobs, and I don't. And, if I'm honest, I like doing it. There's not much work when everybody brings food. It'll be a lovely, friendly occasion.'

Lucy could imagine Alice's grunt, rather than hear it. 'I hope at least they help to wash up.'

Keeping her voice even, Lucy said, 'They always offer, and will probably do the clearing away of everything from the garden, but I prefer to do the washing up myself.' Alice seemed to have got out of bed the wrong side today. Then Lucy realised - she was probably nervous about this date, if her guess was correct. Lucy swiftly moved the conversation on. 'Oh, and this time we've got a special treat. Neil is bringing prosecco for us all.'

'Neil… ah, yes, that's your toy boy, isn't it.'

Now Lucy really had to bite her tongue. 'Neil is hardly older that you, I would say. He's a pleasant man, just finding his feet having moved back to the UK after some years in New York. I've taken him under my wing a bit, and he says I remind him of his mother, who died a few years ago. I've told him all about you.'

'*All* about me? I certainly hope not.' She looked at her watch. 'Anyway, I've got to get ready and go soon. I hope you enjoy your party. And your prosecco.'

It was probably the best point to end the conversation. Their goodbyes were a little more stilted than usual.

When Lucy got up the next morning, she saw that Alice had sent a message. *'Sorry about the toy boy remark earlier. Tbh I was cranky because I was going out on a morning date that I wasn't sure of, first time with this one. Then the bugger didn't show up. I've had it with blokes. Hope you enjoy your party X'*

*

There was never much money in the early years, but Lucy and Kevin managed. Alice was born five months after they got married, and she filled a hole in Lucy's heart that she never knew she had. But it didn't make it any easier, though, that they weren't able to give Alice any brothers or sisters. After the fourth debilitating miscarriage, Lucy and Kevin accepted that their one daughter would have to be enough for them. As Lucy had predicted, they eventually got their own home. Even with Lucy's wages it could be hard to make ends meet, especially since Kevin wasn't the best money manager and tended to have impulsive, extravagant tastes

'We could pawn my ring, you know,' said Lucy one particularly difficult month when there had been some eye-watering repair bills on the car. She fingered the five stones above her gold wedding band, as she was wont to do. 'After all, it was never really mine. You didn't buy it for me.' And I don't really believe all that nonsense about the diamonds bringing good luck to the wearer, she added silently to herself. The picture of her late mother-in-law came in her mind, bleached hair, dirty nails and cigarettes, solemnly presenting her with the ring and saying how it had come down through the family, and that she could remember her grandmother recounting how her grandfather had stolen it from a gypsy. Lucy didn't think her mother-in-law had ever been too much to be relied on.

Kevin didn't answer straight away. He sat at the table in his work overalls, as he often did nowadays. The round, fat teapot sat between them along with three greasy plates, cleared now of the egg, chips and peas that they'd just eaten. Alice was lying on the carpet crooning to herself and colouring in a picture, like the good little girl she was. 'Mam would have hated you getting rid of her heirloom,' he said. He took a big slurp of tea. 'Maybe I can get some overtime. Let's leave selling the ring as a last resort, shall we?'

*

It was funny how 'bring a plate' events always worked. Without any coordination, you never got six plates of chicken or abundant cakes and no savouries. Of course, once you'd done it a couple of times with the same crowd, people started to settle on their own signature dishes. For example, Lucy had previously praised Lesley's homemade hummus with pitta bread, so now you knew what to expect her and Jane to bring. Sarah tended towards sandwiches. Old-fashioned, perhaps, but dependable. Neil, new kid on the block that he was, had ingratiated himself by splashing out on a couple of Marks & Spencer quiches, fancy crisps and the promised prosecco. Carrie and Frank hadn't shown up yet – if they were going to come at all. Lucy, as well as making her famous Welsh cakes, had contributed a varied cheese board with crackers. And a few extra back-ups lurked in her cupboard, 'just in case'. Luckily, the weather had held and the sunshine and circulating wine bottles were contributing to the bonhomie.

'Lucy,' Charlie had come up beside her chair, and fixed his unblinking child's stare on her. 'Can I have a sandwich? Jane says I have to ask you first.'

Lucy found it disconcerting that Charlie called Jane by her name. But then with two mummies, perhaps it was the most sensible thing to do. 'Of course you can. Let's see what type they are, shall we?' Lucy had babysat for Charlie now and again once Covid was over, and she was quite fond of him.

Sarah took a small sip of her wine and watched as Lucy and Charlie probed her sandwich selection. Eventually they settled on ham and her mouth tightened as she saw them pulling out and discarding the tomato slices that she had carefully cut and teamed with the meat. It looked like this boy was going to turn out to be a fussy eater, like most of them did. But there her thoughts on the subject ended abruptly because Neil was approaching her. He moved a chair up next to hers and sprawled in it, legs practically akimbo, like men do, highlighting the tanned thighs protruding from his shorts. She moved her gaze to his face and rearranged her features into a smile.

'Well, this is nice,' said Neil, as he sat down, 'Getting us all together for a gathering. Real neighbourly, I reckon.' He took a glance at Sarah over the rim of his glass. With her hair all fluffed out like that and a little smile playing with her mouth, it confirmed his previous impression that she was really not bad looking. And he liked to be charitable.

'Yes, it's pleasant,' she replied. 'I was able to make time to come this afternoon. I have a lot of marking to do, but I decided it could wait until this evening.'

'You're a schoolteacher, right? You said so when we met briefly met once before, on the stairway. You were just on your way to work, I think.'

So, he remembered, did he?

*

'It still feels strange, being invited to a residents' do where I'm just the odd job man and the gardener. It don't feel right to me.' Frank clutched the carrier bag on his lap containing their contribution to feast. Or rather Carrie's, since she had bought and prepared it all for both of them.

Carrie brought the car to a halt at the red traffic light. 'I know it's not usual, Uncle Frank, but Lucy seems to have taken it on herself to socialise everyone in The Beeches and make them into a unit. It's rather charming, I think. And it's kind of her to have included us, so let's just be grateful, eh?'

Frank grunted. 'I suppose so. Let's see, I know this Lucy. She's the old biddy who always brings me a cup of tea when I'm doing the garden. Yes, she's a good sort alright. Who else is going to be there?'

'Just the other tenants, I guess. Sarah's been there the longest, then there's Jane and Lesley with little Charlie who have the biggest flat, and a man called Neil who's only been renting for a few weeks. I think you said you met him.' While Frank was digesting this she added, 'By the way, when you come to do the garden at The Beeches this week, could you see what you think about a bit of external painting, perhaps in the autumn? It's starting to look like it needs a freshen up. It's been a few years since it's been done.' Carrie flicked on the indicator and slowed to turn into The Beeches forecourt.

'I can start the job before the autumn if you like. I could certainly do with the extra money.'

'Couldn't we all,' replied Carrie. She turned the engine off and pulled down her mirror on the back of her driver's sun visor to check her hair and lipstick. Whereas she enjoyed her job as an estate agent, she had hoped for a substantial promotion by now, with a pay rise to go with it, such as head of the Branch. As it was, she headed up Property Management, which included looking after quite a big portfolio of properties. Of all these, The Beeches had become her favourite, not least because of the people who lived there. Look at the way Lucy had made her own informal little Residents' Association, and she'd been kind enough to invite her and Frank to this one.

It was certainly blatant nepotism that she had wangled the post of freelance handyman and gardener for Uncle Frank. But the appointment was within her power, and it was scarcely a high-profile role, after all, and Uncle Frank was grateful, after he'd been widowed. Carrie got out of the car and shut the door. Presumably all the residents were going to be there this afternoon. Including that rather nice man who had moved into the flat next to Lucy's.

*

'Carrie, Frank, I'm so glad you could come!' The delight was clear on Lucy's face. They had stood uncertainly on the edge of the little party waiting for Lucy, the de facto hostess, to welcome them. She gets up slower than she used to, thought Carrie, watching Lucy struggle up from her garden chair. She fussed around, putting their food offerings on the garden table, which served as a buffet, and getting them drinks. 'Carrie, my dear, could you make sure that Frank knows everyone? I'm not sure if he's met Neil yet, and it will be nice for Neil to have another man to talk to. Then we can all start eating this delicious food. I think we need a few more napkins – I'll just go and get some.'

On her way back from her kitchen Lucy paused at the window, her hands full of more napkins and additional forks, in case there weren't enough. It was all going well. The group was drifting towards the food, and the sound of relaxed chatter reached her through the window. Lesley was busy tucking a napkin under Charlie's chin and encouraging him to have something on his plate besides crisps. Jane had joined Neil and Frank at the buffet, and they were exchanging comments and gesticulating towards the spread. Carrie and Sarah were making their way to the table while they seemed to be discussing something quite enthusiastically. It was a pleasing tableau.

I've made this, thought Lucy. Me. I've taken this disparate group of people with their separate lives and made them into a family for a while. My little family. They are all enjoying themselves and getting along. Suddenly she thought of Alice. How proud her daughter would surely be if she could see her now. But Alice was so far away, and unexpectedly Lucy felt tears spring to her eyes. Stop it, she told herself. Why this sudden gloom? She put the napkins and forks down on the worktop and held onto it. It's because I'm not feeling so well, she admitted to herself. I'm trying to ignore it, but I feel tired, a bit dizzy, and sort of heavy. I must be getting old.

*

It was just getting light the next morning when Lucy dragged herself up. She sat on the edge of the bed and took some deep breaths. For the first time she had allowed the others to help with the clearing up. In fact, they had done it all – getting rid of the remaining food, washing the dishes, drying them and putting everything away, while she herself sat in a chair and directed operations. And it had all been an unqualified success; by the end everyone was laughing, and spirits were high. Perhaps she should just take a look round the garden to make sure nothing had been missed. And some air might do her good.

The early morning air was blessedly fresh. It kissed her face with its coolness, and birds in the trees shrilled out their dawn chorus to greet her. The pain came roaring out of nowhere and grabbed at her chest. The paving slabs of the patio seemed to be eating the side of her face, and the inscrutable sky mocked her. She opened her mouth to call for help, but no sound came out, and the black blanket was creeping to envelope her. But wasn't that footsteps beside her? The last thing she was aware of was a hand tugging at hers, tugging until the ring slid from her helpless finger.

Chapter 4

'Eat up your toast, darling. Look, we can cut it up to dip into your boiled egg. When I was a little girl, we used to call the little pieces of toast 'soldiers'.' Jane sliced the bread into egg-sized strips. Charlie was in one of his mutinous moods and was not going to be cajoled into eating his breakfast. Jane and Lesley knew why that was: he was allowed Coco Pops on a weekend morning, but only on one day, as a treat. Lesley, being a dental hygienist, knew better than most that too much sweet food was detrimental to kids' teeth – let alone what it did to the rest of their health.

'With hindsight,' Lesley said to Jane, 'We shouldn't have let him have Coco Pops yesterday morning, given that he was sure to have cake and other sweet stuff at Lucy's party.'

'Mmm,' said Jane neutrally. It was not that she disagreed with Lesley's high standards, but they were a bit hard to live up to sometimes, when you just wanted a quiet life.

Lesley sat down at the table where Jane was doing her best to tempt Charlie with his boiled egg and soldiers. 'What time does your shift start, love?' said Lesley.

'Not until eleven o' clock, so I've got plenty of time.'

'I don't want you to go to work today! I want you to stay at home and we can all go to the park!' Charlie's mouth turned down, and it was clear that tears were not far away.

'But I have to go to work on a Sunday sometimes,' said Jane. You know that I look after poorly people in the hospital. You don't want them to have no-one to look after them, do you?'

Charlie pushed his plate away. 'I don't care about them,' he said. 'I want you to stay here with me.'

'Let me try,' said Lesley. 'Charlie, I'm going to take you to the park this afternoon, and perhaps we can go on the boating lake. And, after you've eaten your breakfast, would you like to take some of your cars into the garden and play on the patio? You wanted to do that yesterday but there were too many people, remember? You could have an adventure in the garden.'

He hesitated. Lesley pressed her advantage. 'Tell you what, you eat half of your egg and soldiers, and you can go to the garden all on your own for a bit then, after a few minutes, I'll come and find you.'

Lesley's eyes met Jane's questioningly, over Charlie's head. Jane looked out of the window. 'The front gate's shut, and we can watch and see that no-one opens it. So it should be OK. Look, isn't that Frank's van parked by the kerb?'

Lesley looked outside. 'Seems like it. He's probably doing next door's garden as well as ours. He doesn't usually come on a Sunday, does he?'

'He seems to come when he wants to. Perhaps he glanced around yesterday and thought it was about time he gave our garden some attention,' said Jane. Charlie was now dipping his toast carefully into his egg, engaged in not letting the yolk drip. The women smiled over his head, both of them relieved that the tantrum had been averted. Lesley was prepared to keep her word about the eat-half-your-breakfast bargain, but having got into the swing of soldier dipping, Charlie ate all of it and then trotted off to get his shoes and a couple of cars. Jane went to change into her nurse's uniform. Lesley felt in her pocket for the letter. She pulled it out with a frown but thrust it back when she heard Jane's footsteps

They dispatched Charlie through the front door with exhortations to be careful and not to make too much noise.

The women looked at each other for a moment. Jane brushed at an imaginary speck of dirt on the front of her uniform. 'He loves the garden, doesn't he?' she said. 'It's just perfect for a kid. You don't want anything too neat and tidy.'

Lesley glanced out of the window and ascertained that the gate was still closed. Frank's van still stood outside. She cleared her throat and pulled the letter out of her pocket. 'This came yesterday from the bank. They are sorry to inform me that there were insufficient funds to meet the payment on the car. She put the letter down carefully on the table. 'Don't worry, I've seen to it. I paid it from my account.'

With a sigh, Jane sat down at the table, and Lesley sat with her and took her hand. 'Thank you, darling,' said Jane. But you shouldn't have to do that. Again.' Jane squeezed her wife's hand. We're never going to be able to afford another child at this rate.'

Lesley reached over and stroked back a strand of hair that had fallen across Jane's face. 'I don't think this is serious. We just seem to have had a lot of expenditure lately. Let's talk about it later, when Charlie's in bed, and see where we could make some savings. It'll be fine.'

Jane allowed herself to be persuaded. 'OK. Anyway, I can't think about it now, I've got to get to work soon. We'd better go and see if Charlie's OK.'

'I'll go if you like.' Lesley stood up and put the letter back in her pocket.

She had got as far as the side of the house when Charlie came running round from the back. 'Come and see,' he said. 'You'll never guess.'

'What, love?' Lesley allowed the excited boy to take her hand and lead the way.

'It's Lucy. She's lay down on the patio and she's fast asleep!'

*

Was it morning? Was it evening? Alice didn't really know anymore and moreover she couldn't be bothered to care. She had completed the first leg of her journey, that is, from Sydney to Singapore. Then she had mooched about for a couple of hours in the terminal lounge along with her fellow passengers bound for London, while the plane refuelled. She had stretched her legs by strolling around aimlessly and sipped at her water bottle to keep up her hydration levels. Somewhat tentatively she had messaged Zoe and Joe and received typically laconic replies. Basically, she had to accept that they were adults and therefore old enough to look after themselves, with their dad in the background.

Alice had been a bit surprised by how both Zoe and Joe didn't have much to say when she broke the news to them that Granny had died. But after all, they only ever saw her face to face once a year at Christmastime, with the occasional video call or message in between. Despite never forgetting their birthdays and being interested in what they did, she had definitely been peripheral to their lives. To them, Great Britain, where their grandmother lived, was a place where there had been a war and they have a Royal Family. They were definitely Aussie through and through like their dad, and no-one ever guessed that their mum was Welsh. They really are remarkably normal kids, thought Alice to distract herself as she sat in the Departure Lounge, one eye on the sign that was going to reveal when they could start the next leg of their journey. Even when Dan and I separated they seemed to take it in their stride and carry on as if not much had happened. It probably helped that Zoe was only fourteen months older than Joe. In fact, people took them for twins sometimes. God, however did I cope with two babies, mused Alice, taking another swig from her water bottle. And now, how neat it is that they've chosen to go to the same university and that they get on so well. They both seemed to leave home and settle in without a backward glance. But after all, that's what I did, thought Alice.

As was typical, after taking her A level exams when she was eighteen, Alice had left home to go to university, just like Zoe and Joe. She had chosen to do her studies in Bristol, so not very far from her home in Wales, in fact. She had got a good degree in biochemistry and so had gone on to do a doctorate, this time in London. Mum must have missed me, thought Alice. I didn't used to go home very much. By the time I was in London, it was only about three times a year. I was too busy having a good time. And working, to be fair. I've never really thought about how it must have been for Mum and Dad's only child to leave home without so much as a backwards look. Then of course soon after that I was lucky enough to get a placement in Sydney, and I never came back to live in the UK. I wish I could talk to Mum about how she felt about me disappearing from her life like that. But I can't now.

Alice's ruminations were cut short by the flashed-up notice that their plane was ready to board again. There was a frenzy of bag gathering and jumping up amongst the waiting passengers, even though they really knew that it was going to take ages to get everyone on board and the plane wasn't likely to go without them. Alice allowed herself to be infected by the surge of activity and joined the rapidly forming queue.

Back inside the aircraft Alice buckled her seat belt in her window seat and tried not to think about the further thirteen hours or so flying time to London. Well, at least my dual Australian/British citizenship should help to speed me through immigration control when I finally get there, she said to herself. There were some advantages to getting hitched to an Aussie bloke, even if the marriage hadn't lasted.

The exhausting flight wasn't all she didn't want to think about. Did Mum really make this arduous journey every year to see her family? It must have been a huge strain at her age, but she always made light of it. Why had the trip for Mum and her to meet never happened the other way round? The thought automatically occurred that she could suggest it when they met, but of course that wasn't going to happen now. She was never going to see her mother again.

Mum, you're not really dead, are you? You can't be. Imaginary conversations with her mum were nothing new to Alice. For much of the twenty years she had been living in Australia, she had been hearing her mother's wise voice in her head, and they would have a dialogue. This practice had probably started around the time when Alice's marriage had broken up. With her mum on the other side of the world, she couldn't just offload to her any time she liked.

No, Alice dear, of course I'm not dead! And I'm so glad you're coming to visit me. We'll have such a nice time together. I'll show you my home and introduce you to my friends… Those were the words that Alice would have so much liked to hear from her mother.

Alice craned her head to see out of the window, and the lights of the city were receding as the aircraft gained height. The two voices in her head started again, but this time it was two Alices speaking, not Alice and her mother. It's not true, there's been some mistake, said the first Alice. She was fine last time we met on Zoom, and she told me she was looking forward to her garden party. I'll get to her flat and find her there, and yes, she'll be surprised to see me. No, you won't, said the other Alice. You'll see her laid on a mortuary slab. And in the last conversation that you had with her you weren't very nice, were you, and now you'll never get the chance…

'Excuse me, would you like a sweet? I find it helps your ears if you suck something until the plane's levelled off.' The pleasant looking woman sitting in the next seat, suntan and friendly smile, was pushing a bag of something sticky towards her.

'No thanks, not for me,' said Alice, trying to be polite.

The woman put the sweets in her capacious bag and stowed it under her seat. 'Oh, you're Australian, are you? We're just on our way home from there. We decided to break the journey with an overnight stopover in Singapore, didn't we, love?' She tried to include her husband, who was in the next seat, in the conversation, but he just nodded and buried his head back in his book. Alice wasn't surprised that the woman had an English accent. Few Australians nowadays let themselves get as tanned as she was.

Alice confirmed that she lived in Sydney. Frankly she hadn't expected the accent she'd acquired over the years to be picked up after just a few words. No doubt she would stick out like a sore thumb in Britain. Not that that would matter. Friendly Lady went on to enthuse about how they had loved their holiday in Australia, a trip of a lifetime for them to celebrate their silver wedding. Alice nodded and made appropriate responses, including agreeing with them about how amazing the Sydney Opera House is.

'Are you going to visit family in the UK?'

Alice stumbled over her answer. Her mum had been her family, apart from a couple of cousins whom she could barely remember. Dad and Mum's brother Uncle Tom had both been dead for a few years, and she'd never kept up with Dad's side.

Friendly Lady was waiting eagerly for Alice's response. She just panicked and blurted out yes; she was visiting family. That was all Friendly Lady needed to start gushing about how nice that will be, where did the family live, and other effusive comments. Alice answered as concisely as she could without being rude and was saved from having to answer any more enquiries by the arrival of the drinks' trolley.

'Good evening, can I get you something to drink?' The flight attendant unobtrusively placed a small pack of snacks and a napkin on Alice's tray. She asked for a double gin and tonic plus a small bottle of wine to have with her dinner afterwards. As expected after a few minutes of sipping her drink the alcohol did its work and she started to feel calmer, helped by the fact that her neighbour had now turned to talk to her husband. Get a grip, ordered the other Alice. There will be plenty of questions when you get to Britain, and you can't go to pieces like that every time you have to handle one. Alice finished the rest of her drink in a gulp and swirled the still unmelted ice cube round in her plastic glass. There will be all sorts of legal admin, the funeral to arrange and Mum's stuff to sort. Not for the first time, Alice wished she had some siblings. And as for grieving, what was that? She felt she hadn't even started yet.

Dinner arrived, even though it was now well past midnight. Mercifully it seemed that Friendly Lady must have decided that Alice wasn't the talkative type, so she and her husband chatted instead. Alice mechanically worked her way through all the food in the little plastic containers, eating the salad, chicken pasta, bread roll and chocolate dessert, even though she couldn't say she was very hungry. She swallowed her over-the-counter sleeping pill with a swig of her wine and refused the coffee that was offered. There would be a lot that she had to face and to do tomorrow, and she would need all her strength. The cabin lights dimmed, and Alice slept.

*

The Heathrow Express train had whisked Alice past bleary views of grey London suburbs and disgorged her and her luggage on the platform at Paddington Station. Although it was past the main morning rush hour, some later commuters hurried past her with briefcase in one hand and mobile phone in the other. She, by comparison, took her time wheeling her suitcase into the cavernous atrium and scanning the information boards for the right train. She steeled herself to brave the ticket machine, which, as it turned out, accepted her credit card without any difficulty and with relief she saw her ticket eject from the machine.

There was some time to kill before her train, so a few minutes later she was ensconced in the corner of a coffee shop stirring sugar into her double espresso. She hoped this would kick-start her sluggish brain and help her to get to grips with the tasks ahead. And perhaps the numbness and disorientation she felt were no bad things for now. They were keeping the grief at bay so that she could function.

The first thing she had to do was to get in touch with the person who represented the company from whom Mum rented her flat. Already she had exchanged several messages with a woman called Carrie, and they'd arranged that Alice would ring when she knew, approximately, what time she would be arriving at the flat. She dialled the number and listened to the unfamiliar ringing tone.

'Hello… er, hello, can I speak to Carrie please. It's Alice Smith. She'll know what it's in connection with.'

'Hello Alice – is it OK if I call you Alice? It's Carrie here. First, let me say how truly sorry I was about your mother's death. This must be awful for you. And you've come all this way so quickly.'

Alice murmured her thanks. At least this Carrie person didn't ask how she was feeling. She seemed nice enough, though. Carrie went on to tell her that unfortunately she couldn't be there in person today to greet her, but the key for her mother's apartment would be in the key safe by the door, and she would message her the code now.

'If you need any help our gardener, Frank, will probably still be around. I can confirm that since the rent has been paid in advance for another full month, it will be OK for you to stay in the flat for that time. I know you'll have a lot on your hands, clearing it all out and other admin. If I can give you any help or advice, you've only got to ask.'

Once again Alice thanked her. Clearing the flat? Get rid of all Mum's clothes, photographs, books? She hadn't even begun to think properly of that.

*

The door pushed aside a few items of mail as Alice let herself into the Garden Flat in The Beeches. She manoeuvred her case into the small hall and picked up the post. The door into the living room was open and Alice went in. She dropped the mail on the table and stared around her slowly. There was a novel on the coffee table with a bookmark in it. Under the side table next to the sofa lay the *Radio Times*, which Alice saw was open to last Sunday. Both Mum and Dad had always been avid readers of the *Radio Times*, she remembered. She had thought she would know this room from all the Zoom calls, but of course Mum had only shown her around the layout just after she had moved in. The flat felt more than empty, as if it knew its inhabitant hadn't just popped down the road to the shop. The kitchen led off the living room, its clean and tidy work surfaces silent, abandoned. It was almost unbearable.

She opened the window to let in some fresh air. She saw an elderly man in the garden, snipping with shears at a bush. The sound of the window being pushed open must have alerted him because he looked up and right at her. Alice paused. Well, he had seen her now, and she supposed she should go and introduce herself, especially with this not being her flat. Better to get it over with.

The warm summer breeze was welcome after all the hours of travelling, as was the trickling sound of a small river. The man, who must be the gardener mentioned by Carrie, stopped his rather ineffectual trimming and looked at her with what seemed like embarrassment.

'Hello, I'm Alice,' she said. 'I'm guessing you're Frank.'

After a slight hesitation Frank took off his gardening glove and offered her his rather sweaty hand to shake. 'I'm sorry to hear about your mum, love. She was a grand lady, was Lucy.'

Alice realised she would have to hear this phrase, or something very like it, over and over again. They stood awkwardly, both wanting to end the exchange but not sure how to do it.

'Just over there, that's the place.' Frank indicated a spot on the patio.

'I'm sorry? What place?'

'That's where they found her, the two girls from the front flat, it was, in the morning. Don't know how long she'd been there, but she was gone alright. Just like that, God rest her soul.'

Chapter 5

Alice had only been back in the Garden Flat a few minutes when there was a discreet knock at the door. The woman on the doorstep introduced herself as Jane from the front flat, and then there was the condolences exchange that Alice was starting to get used to, and Jane asked if she might come in.

'I'm sorry to intrude on you when you've only just got here and must be exhausted,' said Jane when they were both settled in the living room. 'Carrie messaged me that you'd arrived, and there's a few things I need to sort out with you, pretty much as soon as possible.' Alice registered that Jane's whole demeanour was quiet and soothing yet, at the same time, quite business-like.

'Let me tell you about what I know about your mother's death. My wife Lesley found her lying on the patio at about 9.30 last Sunday morning and came straightaway to get me. I should explain that I'm a hospice nurse, and it was clear to both me and Lesley that Lucy was dead. I arranged to get the medical certificate confirming her death, which is here.' She passed the piece of paper to Alice, who stared at it and tried to focus on the words. 'Basically, it means that your mother had a massive heart attack. I daresay you knew she'd had underlying heart problems for a while.'

Alice hadn't known. Mum had kept this from her. She licked her dry lips before she attempted to speak. 'Did she… I mean had she been lying there all night?'

Jane shook her head. 'No. The time of death was confirmed by a doctor as being very early in the morning. Plus, she was not wearing the clothes she had worn to her party the previous day, nor was she wearing her nightdress.' When Alice continued to gaze at the certificate Jane added gently, 'Alice, as next of kin you need take this certificate and go to register your mother's death, and it really should be today.' When Alice still didn't reply Jane stood up and said, 'But before anything else, let's have a nice cup of tea. I've bought some milk, and I'm sure I can dig out some biscuits and sugar.'

Alice sat back in her mother's armchair and allowed herself to be ministered to. She was doing her best, in her jetlagged and shocked state, to grapple with all the things being thrown at her. While the water was boiling, Jane poked her head round the door and said, 'You'll need to take a taxi to the Registrar's. I would have been happy to take you, but I'm collecting our son from school today.' Then there were homely sounds coming from the kitchen: the opening of cupboard doors, the click of the kettle switching itself off, the chink of crockery. Jane came in carefully carrying a laden tray. There was a tea pot, two cups and saucers (Mum never had been very keen on mugs), a matching milk jug and sugar basin. The whole works, in fact. Also on the tray was an old-fashioned biscuit barrel. It was made of a dark wood and had a crack in one side. The lid, handle and a decorative shield on the front were made of a silvery looking metal.

'The biscuit barrel! We had that when I was a child.' Alice put her hand out and touched the smooth wood grain.

'Well, I never. And Lucy was still using it to keep her biscuits in. Look!' Jane took the lid off and held it out so Alice could see the shortcakes piled inside. There never used to be anything as posh as shortcake. The biscuit barrel used to be filled with common or garden rich tea biscuits, with garibaldi, now and again, as a treat.

It was too much for Alice, that link straight back into her past, when her mother represented security and was always going to be there. She had barely covered her face with her hands before she started sobbing quietly.

*

A few days later Jane was turning her car into The Beeches when she saw Sarah get off the bus where it stopped just past their gate. By the time Jane had picked up her bag from the back seat, Sarah was walking into the drive. Oh well, thought Jane, I don't really need small talk after that long shift, but there's no way I can duck discreetly into my flat now. So she pinned a smile to her face as she got out of the car.

'Warm, isn't it?' said Jane. 'They promised rain, but it didn't come! I shall certainly be glad to get my uniform off and dive in the shower.'

Sarah agreed about the hot day. 'And it's not as if we have any air conditioning in school. Just a fan in the staff room. All the children were restive today. But it's getting towards the end of term so that's usual anyway.' She put her bag of books down on the tarmac and let the bag rest against her leg.

Jane eyed the bag. Seeing it put down did not bode well for a hasty retreat into her flat, a cool drink and that shower. The sweat had welded her uniform to her back after sitting in the car.

'Do you know when Lucy's funeral is going to be? Only Carrie said she would let me know and she hasn't,' said Sarah.

'Oh? She's probably been busy. Anyway, it's next Monday, 2pm at the Crematorium.'

'That soon? That means I won't be able to come, because it's still term time. Isn't there going to be a postmortem?'

Jane locked her car. 'It wasn't necessary. Lucy had been seeing her doctor quite regularly recently because of an ongoing heart condition. That means the funeral can go ahead without a postmortem.'

'You would know about such things, I suppose, in your job.' Sarah made no move to pick up her bag of books. 'I believe her daughter from Australia is here, living in her flat for a month.'

Why does she always manage to irritate me slightly, thought Jane. I mustn't let her. We are neighbours, after all. 'That's right. Her daughter Alice came here as soon as she could and is making all the funeral arrangements. She's very shaken, of course, as you would expect. Have you met her yet? She seems to want to know her mother's neighbours and what her life was like.'

Sarah picked up her bag at last and slung it on her shoulder. She was wearing sandals and Jane was surprised to glimpse bright pink nail polish on her toenails. It seemed out of character, somehow. But then, I don't really know this woman, she thought.

'No, I haven't met her,' said Sarah. 'I expect I should go round and pay my respects before the funeral. Well, goodbye.'

Jane pushed open the door of her flat. 'I'm back,' she called. Charlie and Lesley both came surging out of the living room, probably involved in some manic game. Yes, I'm home, she thought.

*

Could it really be only a week since I arrived here, thought Alice as she came in, flopped down on the sofa and kicked her shoes off. And I never knew that Mum had so many friends! So many people wanting to express their condolences, so many times for me to nod gravely and thank them. And all the stories for me to hear about Mum living her day-to-day life, a life I never really knew. Well, I think I've covered the last of her associates and friends now to let them know about the funeral. All the arrangements seem to be in hand. Dimly, Alice knew that much of the long journey of grieving still lay ahead, and as yet there had been little chance to unpack the carefully guarded pain that was inside her. A friend of Mum's had told her about a bereavement charity that had a helpline offering emotional support. You could just ring anytime to chat about your loss. Alice filed it away in her mind, under 'just in case'.

Alice sat quietly and calmed her breathing. Here she was, staying in Mum's home. You'd think she would feel close to her mum and be able to talk to her like she used to. It was only ever imaginary, after all, those conversations in my head, thought Alice. So why should it be different now? I don't know where she is, but I believe she's somewhere. Perhaps she really does hear my thoughts now, in a way that she didn't when she was alive. Alice tried to tune in, to reach out to her mum. But all she could think about was the one question that she really wanted to ask: Mum, why didn't you tell me that you had heart problems and that you were having treatment? I would have been more prepared then.

Dinner. Alice supposed she ought to think about getting something to eat. She certainly didn't feel like going out again, so she padded out to the kitchen and opened the freezer. She had been surprised by how well stocked her mother had kept it; there was a selection of ready-to-cook meals to choose from. What also surprised her was that many of the meals were for two people, which presumably was more a matter of economy rather than that she often shared the meal with a second person. Or perhaps not? She had all these friends, after all. In her mind's eye Alice could see her bustling around the kitchen, perhaps humming as she prepared her vegetables. An unbidden memory of Sunday lunches when she was young slid into her head. In those days it seemed to take hours for her mother to baste the meat, mash the potatoes, boil the sprouts. Then there was the whole ritual of frenetically stirring the gravy so that there wouldn't be the failure of lumps in it. Alice remembered this clearly, along with her memories of the delicious smell wafting through the house, the leg of lamb sitting proudly on the meat tray while Dad carved it, and Mum dashed in distractedly from the kitchen bearing the accompanying dishes. And then they would sit down and enjoy the bounty. Afterwards they would all be replete and Mum would at last relax. Did I ever tell her that I appreciated her efforts?

Alice clamped shut the door in her mind before that train of thought went any further. She rooted through the freezer and chose a nice rich-looking shepherd's pie. Then she set the oven to heat and hesitantly picked up a bottle of wine. Well, why not? She certainly felt like she'd earned it. She had just filled her glass and taken a glug, feet up on the coffee table, when she heard a knock at the door. She froze in mid swig. Who on earth was that? Maybe if she kept quiet, they'd go away. But the knocking came again, a bit louder this time, so Alice felt she'd better get it over with and went barefooted to answer the door.

Straightaway she guessed who the man was, the one standing there on the doorstep clutching a bunch of flowers. Her mother had described him, right down to his curling hair and suave good looks.

Since he'd brought her flowers, it would have been bad manners not to invite him in. So they did their introductions, Neil's stammered condolences and Alice's appreciation for the posy, in the living room. 'Do sit down while I put these in water,' said Alice. He sat on his edge of the chair clasping his hands together and averted his gaze from the opened wine bottle, or so it seemed to Alice, so of course she had to offer him a glass. Or would he prefer something else?

They sipped their wine. Neil cleared his throat. 'Your mom was very popular here at The Beeches, and none of us can believe it that she died in the way she did, after her party. You probably knew about her parties. They were the best. And she was kind and a good neighbour to me, always hospitable, never complaining or trashing anyone. She really helped me when I first moved in and was a bit lost.'

It was so obviously a rehearsed speech, delivered stiffly and awkwardly, that Alice unbent towards him, putting aside that she'd had enough of people that day. And he had said such nice things about Mum. 'Thank you, I appreciate your kind words. She had mentioned you, of course. How you would come round and eat her legendary afternoon tea with her.' It was getting easier with each day for Alice to put her sadness and bewilderment on the back burner while she said the right things.

'Ah yes,' said Neil, smiling. 'Her Welsh cakes and those cute little sandwiches.' He leaned back in his chair and his shoulders visibly relaxed. 'And she always looked forward so much to her Zoom visits with you every Friday evening – that was Saturday breakfast time with you, right?'

Alice was part touched but also a bit nonplussed that he knew of the weekly chats with her mother. They were private. Surely Mum wouldn't have reported what they'd talked about? She cast about for something to change the subject. 'And are you settled in here now? I must say it seems like a very pleasant place to live.' She shifted position slightly in the corner of the sofa that she had adopted for her own.

'It's great. I couldn't ask for anything better. I work mainly from home, you see, so it's nice and peaceful but convenient to get downtown when I need to. I'll be coming to Lucy's funeral, of course. I wouldn't miss it for the world.' His hands were dangling loosely off the arms of his chair as he sank into it now, his posture radiating ease. I can see why Mum took to him, thought Alice. He's a charmer, alright. Neil went on to say how quickly Alice had got here from Australia. She told him, somewhat mechanically because she had recited the same spiel often now: there had not been much to arrange back home, the kids were away at university, and her employer where she worked as a research assistant was cool about her taking a few weeks off, part compassionate leave and part holiday. 'So I just booked my ticket and came. I think I was on autopilot, though.' And I still am, she added to herself.

'Yeah. It's tough for you alright. Carrie says you're good here for the rest of the month. I guess you've got stuff to sort out, right? I remember when my mom died the admin tasks seemed never ending.'

Alice realised she was probably the subject of gossip and speculation among the residents and associates of The Beeches. She was saved from answering by an insistent beeping from the kitchen to signify that her shepherd's pie was ready. 'You'll have to excuse me,' she said, backing away towards the kitchen. He took the hint, standing up and saying that he had thought something was smelling nice. She made her decision as she was pulling the bubbling pie out of the oven. Well, it was a meal for two after all, and she felt that she was making the neighbourly gesture that her mother would have made. So it ended up with Neil and Alice sitting at her mother's kitchen table with the pie and another bottle of wine between them.

It's true that conversation and conviviality come in bottles, thought Alice, barriers coming down and a familiarity between them gradually taking hold as the wine diminished. They talked all around the edges of Lucy's existence while taking care not to steer too close to her sudden death.

Neil said, 'You know, your mom really was good to me when I first moved in here. Things were challenging for me – well, you don't need to hear the whole story, but I'd just moved back from the US, mainly because of a bad break-up. And Lucy… she seemed to sense that I wasn't in a very good place. She didn't pry or anything, but she was just there, just supportive, you know? Like my own mom would have been.' He put his hands over his face and Alice was dismayed to see that he was on the verge of tears. Alice laid her hand on his arm, feeling helpless at this sudden turn of events.

'Oh my God, I'm like, so sorry!' Neil took a couple of deep breaths and wiped his fingers across his eyes. 'You've just lost your mom, and here's me breaking down like that! Oh my God, I can't believe I just did that!' He pushed his chair back, gasping, got up from the table and strode to the window.

Alice tactfully busied herself collecting the plates from the table and depositing them near the sink. 'It's OK,' she said, feeling inadequate. 'I'll make some coffee, shall I?'

She carried the steaming cups into the living room and allowed Neil to follow her in his own time.

He seemed to have recovered. 'So, are you all set for the funeral?' he said. 'The day after tomorrow, isn't it?'

She nodded. 'I think it's all sorted. I've never done this before, but the undertaker's have been really efficient fixing everything up. Jane put me on to this firm, and they certainly know how to do their stuff.'

'Jane, sure. That figures. Part of her job, I suppose. Have you met all the folks here now?'

'I haven't met the lady in the flat above yours. Sarah, isn't it? I haven't managed to catch her, but I've put a note through her door about the funeral. I call you lot 'The Beeches Crew'. Even Carrie and her Uncle Frank have paid their respects.'

'I'm sorry I left it so long to call on you. But I was kinda dreading it, you know? But now I'm glad I've come. You are like your mom, you know, Alice.'

After she had shown him out, Alice sat again in the darkening living room for a few minutes. What an unexpected evening. And strangely comforting.

*

Alice stared at her phone. She had keyed the number in; she just hadn't pressed the call button yet. She was vaguely aware of summer leaves fluttering slightly outside the window. Mum's friend, who had given her the number, had said that the helpline staff were very understanding and kind, but what would she say, exactly? She realised she was only getting more nervous the longer she hesitated, so she gritted her teeth and connected the phone call. A soft recorded male voice told her that she was in a queue and would be answered as soon as possible. Ten minutes, thought Alice, I'll give it ten minutes.

It was after about seven minutes of anodyne music and Alice drumming her fingers on the table or shuffling round the flat idly touching things that the same voice said 'Thank you for waiting. We're putting you through to a bereavement volunteer now.' The voice changed to that of a middle-aged sounding woman who introduced herself as Daisy and asked how she might help.

Alice's speech deserted her, and all she could seem to do was mumble incoherently.

'Take your time,' said Daisy. 'I'll just wait until you're ready.'

After several deep breaths to control the tears that were threatening, Alice managed to stammer out 'It's my mum. She's died. It was such a shock.'

'I'm so sorry to hear that. I take it that it was unexpected, then?'

The disembodied voice was full of compassion and Alice clutched at it. 'Yes, yes it was. I'd only been talking with her on Zoom the day before, and she sounded fine. Then I had the phone call, so I dropped everything and just came on first flight I could. I live in Australia, you see. Work has been brilliant about time off…' Alice realised she was gabbling, but Daisy allowed her to do just that while she recounted making the long journey to Mum's flat, hearing how she died and was found, making a start on sorting out her stuff and planning the funeral which was tomorrow.

Daisy let her tell her story in her own way and only interjected if part of Alice's narrative needed to be clarified. Finally, Alice said,

50

'Only a short while ago I was going along, living my life in the normal way, a Zoom call with Mum once a week and then suddenly, wham! I'm on the other side of the world thrust into this. I feel... I feel... Oh, I don't know how I feel. It's like a bad dream. Tomorrow is her funeral. And I never even got to say goodbye. I'm dreading the funeral, absolutely dreading it...' Alice's voice trailed off.

'What a challenging time you're having. It's hard enough having a parent die unexpectedly, without having a dash halfway across the world on top of everything. Do you have any brothers and sisters you can share the burden with?'

Alice confirmed that it was just her. 'I did have an uncle, but he's dead now, and I haven't kept up with my cousins, nor with my father's side. He died a few years ago. It's hard to explain how I feel, being here.'

'Do you mean being in Britain?'

'No, I don't mean that. Although since I emigrated, I've only been back once, which was a short trip for Dad's funeral. I meant being in Mum's flat. Did I mention that the landlord has allowed me to stay there until the end of the month? So I'm surrounded by Mum's things, that I've got to clear out of the flat, but Mum's not here. She used to show me round her rooms in our Zoom conversations, but now it's like I've sort of stepped inside through the Zoom image into this other world, and frankly it's weird. It's surreal. And I keep coming across stuff from my childhood that I'd totally forgotten about. It's freaking me out.' The biscuit barrel flashed into her mind.

'I can understand how difficult that must be, especially since I imagine that you have to clear the flat quite quickly?'

'That's right. Mum's friends and neighbours are being really helpful, though. It's so moving, and sort of comforting, to know how popular she was.' Alice talked on, cautiously gaining confidence because she felt that the disembodied voice on the other end of the phone was truly hearing her. She began to weigh up if she could say what was really troubling her to this person who was being so empathetic. Eventually she said, 'I just feel so guilty though...' She paused, not sure how to go on.

'Do you want to tell me what you feel guilty about?'

Alice stumbled, not able to find the words now that she had brought the opportunity about. Daisy waited.

'You see, I found her medications from the doctor, in the bathroom cabinet. She was on all sorts of tablets for her heart. Her friends knew she had some trouble and had undergone tests, but I, her daughter, just didn't know. She didn't tell me. When I asked her if she was OK, she always said yes, and I took her word for it. But I should have known!' Alice felt her voice breaking and she didn't try to stop the tears.

Daisy allowed her to cry. Then she said, 'I get it. That must have been an awful shock for you. But have you thought, perhaps your mum made the choice not to tell you so that you wouldn't be worried, what with you living so far away? That strikes me as being a real act of love.'

Alice considered. She felt the ring of truth in what Daisy had said and allowed herself to take some comfort from it. 'I did love my mum very much, you know. Even though I chose to make my life on the other side of the world because my kids were born there.' Alice talked some more about her life in Australia, then she said, 'There's something else I feel guilty about. It's about the last Zoom conversation I had with Mum, just before she died. Well, I was a bit sarcastic and edgy. Unusually so. To be honest I was nervous about a morning date I had arranged with someone I'd met online, so when Mum made some comments about how I was dressed, I overreacted and made some snide remarks. I didn't know that was going to be the last conversation I'd ever have with her. Later I did message her and apologise, though.'

Once again Daisy responded with understanding. Although it didn't change what had happened, Alice felt consoled by getting it off her chest to someone who wasn't going to judge her.

'Since I've lived away, I have made a habit of having conversations with Mum in my head. Would it be weird if I still did that, even though she's now dead? It's just that, I can't seem to talk with her now. I think maybe it was because she hadn't told me about her heart problem, but well, you've helped me there.'

'It's not at all weird to have a conversation with someone who's died. It can be very therapeutic. Also, for some people it helps to write a letter to the dead person and even to write the reply that you would like to have received. Anything that you can do to comfort yourself, as long as it doesn't hurt anyone else, is OK.' Daisy paused to allow Alice to digest this, then she said, 'I believe you told me your mother's funeral is coming up. Is that right?'

Alice told her that it was tomorrow and that she was dreading it. 'I'm the chief mourner. I'm scared that I'm going to cry and make a fool of myself. I've written a eulogy, but the celebrant is going to read it. I couldn't possibly do that.'

'That sounds like a good decision. And yes, you may well cry. It's perfectly OK if you do. A funeral is a chance to say a formal goodbye, along with other people who knew your mum well, and emotions can safely be released. It's a special time when you can honour and celebrate your mum's life in its entirety, but of course there will be sadness too. Nobody actually looks forward to a funeral. Remember you will be among people who liked or loved your mum, and who will be feeling nothing but sympathy for you. Let them support you.'

Alice digested Daisy's words and felt supported by the reassurance that they offered. She was a whole lot calmer than she had been before she made the call.

'Tomorrow is probably going to be difficult,' said Daisy. 'But look at how well you've done so far. You've shown courage, you know, travelling halfway around the world and taking on all these responsibilities on your own. You can do this. Most people feel considerable relief once the funeral has happened.'

The comfort that Alice felt was enormous. 'Thank you so much. I feel lighter now. I think I can cope.'

Daisy assured her that she would certainly be able to cope and asked if there was anything more it would help her to say right now. Alice couldn't think of anything else, so Daisy brought the call to an end by telling Alice that she could call back another day if it would be useful to chat again.

Alice spent a few minutes staring at the phone and gathering her emotions. What an amazing charity, she thought. I feel calmer now.

Daisy's right, I can do this, and it doesn't matter if I cry at my mother's funeral. She went to the wardrobe and took out the outfit that she had brought with her specially for the event, a grey silk dress, and hung it on the door.

*

Alice opened her eyes and allowed them to adjust to the half-light of the bedroom. Her mother's curtains weren't the blackout type, so the morning light was filtering in through their flimsiness. Rolling over onto her back, she stared up at the ceiling where the light fixture with its energy-efficient bulb and floral lampshade were dimly outlined. She was aware that she felt different this morning. What was it? She lay, allowing herself to surface totally from sleep. Then she had it. Relief. It was over. The funeral was over, and it had gone off well, with no hitches. She had been able to put the mask on and played her part as chief mourner. Throughout the entire event there had been dignity and respect, with no wailing or histrionics, which would have been hard to cope with.

She had chosen to come back to The Beeches on her own, feeling overwhelmed and exhausted from the trying day. Once she was in the flat with the door locked and her pyjamas on, it didn't take long for the tears that she had withheld all day to fall, and once she'd started she couldn't stop. Eventually she cried herself to sleep and, when she woke up briefly a few hours later, her cheeks and eyelids were stiff from dried tears.

Now the night had passed and with it came a certain feeling of peace. She had a thousand and one things to do – Mum's will, notifying various organisations, clearing the flat – but today she had the notion that she would benefit from a break, a day off. Some exercise would be good. A nice long walk on her own and a pub lunch by the river, for instance.

With that thought to encourage her, she got out of bed, opened the curtains and saw that Frank was busy in the garden. It was just after nine o'clock. She drifted out of the bedroom to get on with her morning routine. She didn't see it at first. It was only after she was dressed that the saw a small blank, sealed envelope on the hall floor, in front of the letter box. Puzzled, she picked it up and felt a small item inside. She tipped it onto her palm. It was the diamond ring that she had seen so many times before on Mum's finger.

Chapter 6

In the winter, Kevin usually lit the coal fire in the front room. By the evening, the licking flames had given way to red embers in the grate, so that you could sit quite close to the hearth without scorching yourself. Sometimes there would be washing airing on a clothes-horse nearby, and then the fireguard would be firmly in place, like it always used to be when Alice was a toddler.

Other times, when there was no washing that needed to be dried, Lucy and Kevin would sometimes make toast. They had a toasting fork with an extending handle that they had acquired from goodness knows where. Usually, it was Kevin who sat cross-legged on the hearth rug and speared the thickly cut slice of bread, then held it over the fire. When both sides were golden brown – or dark brown if Kevin lost concentration – he dropped the piece on a plate and Lucy slathered it with butter. This was toast at its best: the outside crisp and hot while the inside was still soft but warm. Alice was the last in the little production line, and it was her job to dollop jam on the buttered slices. She had a tray to work on, to keep the inevitable stickiness contained.

The heavy curtains were closed to keep the dark night out and the warmth of the room in, and they retreated to the three-piece suite to munch on their toast supper. The small room was filled with the smell of the toasted bread, and the glowing coals radiated their comforting heat. For a few minutes the only sound in the room was the ponderous ticking of the clock on the mantlepiece, various bills and other pieces of paper protruding from behind it. Alice, her feet in their pink slippers sticking out over the edge of her seat, cuddled up next to her mother on the sofa.

'Try to keep all the crumbs on your plate, love,' said Lucy, adjusting Alice's plate so it wasn't tilting. Alice obediently tried her best. She licked her fingers to get the last of the jam. 'Mummy, can I have a story?

'I'll read you a story, princess,' said Kevin from his chair next to the fireplace, his long legs stretched out onto the hearth and a cigarette dangling from his fingers. 'How about another from Rupert Bear?'

Alice shook her head. 'Not a reading story, a telling story. Tell the one about the ring again.' She touched Lucy's finger and felt the five stones.

'You like that one, don't you?' said Lucy putting her arm around Alice so they could both snuggle closer. 'Here we go, then. A long, long time ago a man used to go to work every day in the coal mine. It was hard, hard work, deep underground digging away at the precious coal and bringing it out so that people could have it to burn and keep warm by. Just like we are doing right now. Look, Alice, can you see the black coal burning in the fireplace?' Alice stared at the hypnotising red glow. 'What happened next?' she said, although she'd heard the story, with its variants, many times before.

'Well, the man would trudge back home from the coal mine every day, tired, hungry and dirty. It was very black in the coalmine, you see. But even though he was so tired, he always kept a look out for a certain pretty lady he used to see every day. She was walking home from work too, but not from a coalmine. She worked in a shop in the town.'

'What did she look like?' Alice interrupted.

'Oh, she was the prettiest thing the man had ever seen. Her hair was golden, her mouth was pink, and her hands and feet were small and dainty.'

'She looked a lot like you, princess,' said Kevin. Alice wriggled with pleasure.

'So eventually one day the man plucked up enough courage to ask the lady if she would like to go for a walk with him on Sunday, when neither of them had to go to work. And what do you think she said?'

'She said yes! And they went out for a walk again and again, and they held hands, and they kissed, and then they wanted to get married, but the man didn't have much money, and he didn't know what to do…'

'Hey, you really know this story, don't you?' Lucy was laughing as she interrupted Alice and took over the storytelling again. 'Then one day, when he was just getting home from work, there was a gypsy calling at the house trying to sell her wares. The gypsy opened her case and there was a lot of pretty trinkets. The man dearly wished he could afford to get something nice for the lady. Then he saw, in the corner of the case, the most beautiful ring he had ever seen made of no less than one, two, three, four, five diamonds set in gold.' Alice wrapped her fingers around the ring on Lucy's finger.

'The man knew he had to have that ring. So do you know what he did?' Alice shook her head, although she knew the story perfectly well. 'He distracted the gypsy by getting her to look at something in the road, then he quickly picked the ring up and hid it in the palm of his hand. The gypsy didn't see. The man bought something else, a small knick-knack, so the gypsy was pleased and went away.'

'So the man gave the pretty lady the diamond ring and asked if she would marry him. She said yes! Eventually the man had made enough money, so they were able to get a little house, and they had a family and lived happily ever after.'

'And you know who the man and lady were, don't you?' said Kevin.

Alice frowned with concentration. She always got this bit wrong. 'Granny's… daddy?'

'Not quite. The man was Granny's grandfather, and the lady was Granny's granny. And that ring has stayed in our family all that time, and now you can see it on Mummy's finger.'

Alice knew what she had to say next. 'But really, it's naughty to steal. I mustn't do it.'

'That's right, love. But this was a long time ago and perhaps things were different then.' Lucy said as she stroked Alice's hair. 'Now, why don't you go and put your pyjamas on, and I'll be up in a minute.' As Alice was heading upstairs Lucy said to Kevin, 'I do wonder if we should tell that story to the child. After all, it's a bit immoral. And probably made up.'

Kevin got up and stirred the fire with the wrought iron poker which lay on the hearth. 'I don't think so. Mam used to swear that it was true.'

'Yes, but how do we know?'

'Oh, we know. As knowing goes.'

*

It was pleasant on the bench by the side of the river, where people were walking, skateboarding, jogging, cycling by, and the trees nodded in the summer breeze. It would have been the perfect antidote to the stress of the last week if it wasn't for this perplexing conundrum. For the umpteenth time Alice looked down at the ring, which she had placed on her right hand, where it fitted. The diamonds formed a half hoop, with the central diamond being largest and the other two flanking diamonds on each side progressively smaller. All the diamonds were held in place by standard claws. It was certainly a classic piece of jewellery and very familiar to Alice.

As soon as she had tipped the ring onto her palm that morning, she had recognised it. Was it surprising that she hadn't given it a thought since she heard about Mum's death? Probably not, given the shock it had been, plus all she'd had to do. And, to be honest, she hadn't thought about it that much while she was growing up; it was just Mum's engagement ring. It was true that when she was little she liked to hear the story of how the ring came into the family, and that today she had probably made a fairly accurate reconstruction of listening to the tale while she and her parents had sat in the front room and what she may have heard while she climbed the stairs to bed. Her memory of the family legend was strongly linked, as memories often are, to the sensory experiences: the glimmer of the fire, the low resonance of her parents' voices, the stickiness of the jam and, of course, the making and the eating of toast for tea. Ah, freshly made toast from the toasting fork! Your recollections from childhood often serve you falsely, but she was sure that reminiscence was accurate. No electric toaster ever does the job like an open fire and a long-handled fork. Why have I never done that with the kids when we were having a barbie? she thought. Perhaps they would turn their noses up at a humble slice of bread, rough cut and browned. Well, she would try it, as part of their heritage. She had never seen a toasting fork in Australia. Perhaps when she started going through Mum's things she would discover the one from her childhood, still up to the job.

With an effort Alice pulled herself back from the distant past to more recent times. She had never given a thought to the 'family heirloom', as Dad used to call it, when she herself had got engaged. In fact, her romance had been so whirlwind that she didn't have an engagement ring at all, and they had been married just a few weeks later. What a fool I was, thought Alice, not for the first time. But Zoe and Joe had come out of that misbegotten relationship, so it had been worthwhile for that. It was all years ago now. The sun came out, and Alice was flooded with warmth. But it was an unenthusiastic warmth, not the full-bodied heat of a Sydney day in summer. Homesickness unexpectedly washed over her, and she longed to touch base with the kids and be in her own house once more. She wanted to WhatsApp the kids right now, but it was the middle of the night at home, and they would be sleeping.

Meanwhile her work was not yet done here. In fact, she had hardly started on Mum's will and sorting through all her stuff. And now there was this mystery. She frowned in bafflement at the ring, gently feeling the shape of the diamonds under her fingers. Why on earth would someone put the ring through her door without acknowledging themself? Perhaps the person had found it, at the place where she had collapsed maybe, and returned it discreetly. That implied the ring had fallen from her finger. Yes, that was possible. Alice had nearly managed to convince herself of this theory when she remembered something that had happened on Mum's last visit…

They had taken one of their trips to nearby Coogee Beach, famous for its silvery sands and gentle bathing conditions. Mum loved it when on her visits she went in the Pacific Ocean. In fact, they all went in together. But this time there had been an unexpected upset:

Zoe had lost her silver signet ring, a present for her sixteenth birthday, in the waves. Mum had consoled her granddaughter by showing her the diamond ring that would be hers one day, telling her the story of how it was part of family folklore. Zoe had not wanted to be rude, but she said to Alice later that she didn't really want the ring because the story was creepy, even if it was partly or totally made up.

'Do you think you should wear that valuable ring in the ocean?' Alice subsequently said to Lucy. 'After all, look how Zoe's ring just slipped off her finger and, before you knew it, it was gone.'

Mum had said, 'I always take it off when my hands are going into soapy water because I'd heard that detergent or whatever might damage it, but not seawater. Seawater's OK. I don't know if that's very logical. But anyway, look how tight it is on my finger. It can't possibly slip off – I have to pull it off.'

*

'Did Charlie tell you about his friend whose family dog died?' said Jane to Lesley after Charlie had been settled down in bed for the night.

Lesley was curled up on her end of the sofa, a pile of books and general domestic debris on the coffee table in front of them. 'No,' she said without taking her eyes from her phone where she was scanning through Facebook. 'What about it?'

'Well, the boy was upset and Charlie comforted him, apparently. He said that dying means a body stops working because it's got too old, or it got too sick. He told him that every person and every animal have to die sometime, and the dog was very old, so it was his time to die.'

'You don't say?' Lesley put her phone down. 'So he took notice of all that stuff we said when Lucy died – it seems like it's really sunk in. And he was kind to his friend. You know how we're always drumming it into him about kindness. Oh, well done Charlie! Well done, son! Let's give him a special treat tomorrow.'

Jane agreed. 'I was proud of him too.' She hesitated. 'Of course,

Charlie didn't know that Lucy was already dead when he saw her, he thinks she had fallen over and was sleeping and that she died later.'

'We did the right thing, didn't we?' The two women looked at each other and were silent. 'Well, it was best that he was out of the way when the paramedics came.'

Jane glanced at the clock and swung herself upright. 'I suppose I'd better tidy up a bit,' she said, gathering mugs and biscuit wrappers from the coffee table.

'Tidy up?'

'Don't you remember? Alice, Lucy's daughter, asked if she can pop round for a chat. We said come this evening.'

'Oh shit, I'd forgotten.' Lesley ran her fingers through her hair in a half-hearted attempt to comb it. 'What do you suppose she wants?'

'I don't know exactly.' The doorbell sounded, and Lesley got up to answer it, while Jane hurried to the kitchen, laden with the coffee table debris.

Alice sat down where she was invited while the three of them exchanged slightly awkward greetings. She risked a surreptitious look around while Jane and Lesley were getting refreshments in the kitchen. A large old-fashioned fireplace housing a gas fire dominated the room and that, plus the higgledy-piggledy piles of books on the floor, contributed to a homely, lived-in feel. A big pile of toys took up one corner, and a few brightly coloured Lego bricks had spilled out onto the carpet. Alice could hear conversation from the kitchen. Did the mutterings sound urgent? Alice strained her hearing, but she couldn't make out the actual words.

They settled down with their drinks. Alice filled the conversational space with 'I'm guessing your little boy – Charlie, isn't it – is in bed?'

Charlie's two mummies both started to speak together, then Lesley explained that they liked him to be settled in bed quite early during the school week. Alice asked how old he was, and Jane confirmed he was nearly six. 'Your mum used to babysit him sometimes in the last couple of years. He loved seeing her,' she added.

After a pause Alice said 'I wanted to pop round and thank you both for coming to Mum's funeral and, particularly, for taking care of the early stages after she died. Lesley, I believe Jane said it was you who found Mum?' Alice could hear herself being rather direct and formal, but she wanted to get to the point.

Lesley crossed her legs. 'To be totally accurate, it was Charlie who found her. We've let him believe that she was sleeping when he saw her. I went to get Jane, and I think you know the rest.' Alice nodded while Lesley went on to say what a lovely lady Lucy was and what a shock it must be for Alice. 'Lucy was so well liked here at The Beeches.'

Before Alice could nod her acknowledgement, a text message notification sounded on her phone. She wondered fleetingly who that could be, given that it was still night in Australia so unlikely to be from there. However, she didn't want that to interrupt her train of thought. She pressed on. 'This is a slightly awkward subject. When Mum was cremated, she was wearing her wedding ring, but I know she wasn't wearing her diamond engagement ring, and I'm trying to shed some light on why that was. I've been in touch with the undertakers again, and they can confirm that they never saw any engagement ring at all. I was wondering if you had any recollection of seeing it, especially after you found her on the patio? I realise this is a bit of a strange question.'

Alice watched the two women closely as they exchanged inscrutable glances. After some head shaking Jane said, 'Actually I do remember seeing her wearing that ring and thinking that it was rather beautiful. But after she was lying on the patio? I certainly didn't notice then if she was wearing it or not. Did you, Lesley?'

Lesley shook her head. 'As you'll appreciate, we had other things to think about.' In the silence that followed they heard a car turning into the drive.

'Yes, of course, and you were both marvellous. I know it was a long shot, but I just thought it was worth asking.'

Lesley frowned. 'Do you know where the ring is now?'

Alice took a deep breath. 'No, I don't.'

The two women shook their heads and looked grave. Jane said it would probably come to light among her mother's effects.

Alice said she was going to start sorting her mother's things in earnest tomorrow. After a couple more stumbling sentences she took her leave.

So… I didn't learn anything there, but not that I really expected to, thought Alice as the front door closed behind her. And at least one of us was lying, although I managed to keep to the truth apart from that direct question of Lesley's about knowing where the ring is. Alice unzipped the pocket of her jacket and put her hand in to reassure herself that the ring was still there, where she had put it.

*

'Hey, Alice!'

Alice turned around in the carpark to see Neil emerging from behind the boot of his car, slamming it shut and sauntering around with a large pack of beer under his arm and a bulging carrier bag of groceries in his other hand. 'Hello, Neil. I didn't see you there.'

'How are you doing?' You looked like you were deep in thought.' She felt his eyes appraising her. 'I sent you a message not long ago. Did you get it?'

'Oh… did you? I haven't had chance to look at my messages.' She fumbled in her bag for her phone.

'It doesn't matter. I can tell you what was in it now. I want to say thanks for the meal you cooked at your place – well, your mom's place – the other day, so would you like to come out for dinner one evening? We could take the car and go out of town a way, perhaps to a village someplace.'

Alice, feeling somehow wrongfooted, stammered out a reply about it being kind but he didn't need to. She felt that all she wanted right now was to be on her own to mull over the session with Jane and Lesley.

'You'd be doing me a favour, you know. It would be great to chat more about Lucy, and also to find out more about you. How about tomorrow evening?'

Alice felt her resistance weakening. It would be nice to talk about

64

Mum with someone who'd known her a little, also to have an evening out. And, although he was obviously full of male swagger, he couldn't possibly be hitting on her, could he? 'OK. Shall I meet you at seven, in the carpark?

His face lit up with a smile. 'Cool,' he said.

Chapter 7

I really shouldn't procrastinate any longer, said Alice to herself. She'd already indulged in a long shower, a leisurely breakfast accompanied by morning TV, and a stroll around the garden. She had paused and paid her respects, like she had taken to doing, at the spot on the patio where Frank had told her that her mother had been found. But now the connection she had initially felt with her mother's last moments was tainted by the knowledge, or at least suspicion, that a shadowy figure had bent over her and removed the valuable ring from her dead body. It was hard to credit, but that was probably what had happened. Mum would never have given the ring away – it was the family heirloom – and if she had accidentally left it somewhere, why didn't the finder share that information? It didn't make any sense.

Right. I've only got a couple of weeks left in the flat, so I really must get stuck in and start to sift through Mum's stuff, Alice said to herself. She dragged her mind away from the ring conundrum to producing a strategy for her task. There were four rooms plus the small entrance hall and bathroom. So, perhaps I could do one room per day. Yes, that would give me manageable goals. Encouraged by having formulated a plan of action, Alice decided to start in the kitchen, since this was likely to be the least emotionally challenging area.

She started looking through one floor-level cupboard. From inside it she pulled out the biscuit barrel that had so undone her the other day when Jane had been here. And look, here was Mum's traditional bakestone, right at the back! She let her fingers caress its ancient black surface, far older than herself. What am I going to do with these objects which hold part of my childhood? she thought. I can't keep them, and I certainly can't take them back home with me. That friend of Mum's suggested a local charity that would take these things. I'll have to follow up on that.

Alice opened a drawer, not the one which contained neat rows of cutlery, but the other one, found in every kitchen, stuffed with such necessary items as rolls of cling film, Sellotape, scissors, bottle openers, and the like. I can just get rid of all this, thought Alice. But wait a minute… at first, she saw only the handle, so she pulled it out of the drawer and gasped in utter amazement. The toasting fork! Now why on earth would Mum have kept that? She had no open fire here in the flat, so it must have been pure nostalgia. The toasting fork, with its extendable handle, was an item that was slim and relatively light, so it was definitely going in her suitcase to Sydney. It would feature in her next barbie with the kids. She fantasised the scene. She would unveil the fork with a flourish, Zoe and Joe would initially be puzzled by this implement, then bowled over and open mouthed with amazement when she showed them how they could make perfectly toasted buns to accompany their burgers. Finally, they would be even more lost in wonder when she told them it had belonged to their grandparents.

Yeah, right. In your dreams, Alice, she said to herself, with a wry smile. Maybe she'd just keep the toasting fork as a memento. Nevertheless, she felt more grounded now, both by finding such a potent reminder of Mum and also by her imagined barbie. So she got on and efficiently reviewed the rest of the kitchen, mainly crockery and pots and pans, which didn't carry any emotional charge. All this stuff could be easily disposed of.

I can tick the kitchen off my list of rooms for sorting, she thought with some satisfaction when she went to get changed for her evening out a couple of hours later. She surveyed her outfit options carefully and decided that jeans and a blouse would strike the safe note she was aiming for, even more so if she didn't wear any make-up. Perfume? Definitely not. Before she left the flat, at five minutes to seven, she hesitated and frowned again at the message she'd received from Carrie while she had been getting changed. I'll answer it tomorrow, she thought.

*

When Alice went round to the front of The Beeches, Neil was already there talking to an unknown woman. Alice judged she was a bit younger than herself. The person had neat fair hair cut chin length and was wearing a light raincoat over a dress. She had a plastic carrier bag in her hand. She and Neil were chatting amiably and surveying a car, one that Alice hadn't seen before that was parked next to what Alice assumed was Neil's car. His face broke into a smile when Alice's presence had been announced by the crunch of her footsteps on the gravel of the driveway. He was wearing a stylish tee shirt and jeans, so Alice felt comfortable in her choice of outfit for the evening.

'Hi, Alice,' he said. 'Good to see you. How are you doing?'

Her reply was conventional. 'I'm fine, thanks, and nice to see you too.' She glanced at the raincoated woman, and Neil took his cue. 'Have you met Sarah?' he said. 'She lives in the flat above mine.'

Both women shook their heads and murmured their hellos, slightly warily perhaps. Alice extended her hand and, after a slight hesitation, Sarah shook it briefly. 'I'm Lucy's daughter,' said Alice, since Neil hadn't explained. 'Mum mentioned you, Sarah.'

'My condolences on the death of your mother,' said Sarah, with the awkwardness that Alice had got used to hearing. 'I'm sorry that I wasn't able to come to her funeral, but I was teaching, you see.'

'Of course, I understand. Did you know Mum well?' Alice injected warmth into her voice.

'No, not really. I tend to keep myself to myself, you know. But we were neighbours, and I used to go to the gatherings that she kindly organised. They were pleasant.'

'I was just admiring Sarah's car that she's just recently bought,' said Neil, running his hand over its bonnet. 'The Mini sure is the classic little car – perfect for local journeys.' It was only slightly patronising, since Neil's own car was a sporty model that Alice didn't know the name of. Sarah's car looked like a toy next to it.

'I've wanted a little car for a while now, mainly, you know, to travel to work, and recently I found myself in a position to get one,' said Sarah. Alice's antennae quivered at this enigmatic comment. Was this Sarah woman in such a position because she had just sold an expensive ring? No, of course not. The ring has been returned to me, you fool, she thought. Get a grip, will you.

'Well,' said Neil, turning to Alice and pulling his keys from his pocket to unlock the car, 'Shall we?'

'It's been nice to meet you,' said Alice to Sarah as she went round to the passenger door. 'I do hope we'll get chance for a proper chat before I go home.'

Before Sarah could reply Neil said, 'Say, we're just going out for a bite to eat. Why don't you join us? It's only to a pub on the edge of town. Nothing fancy.'

Alice felt her friendly expression freeze while she waited for Sarah's reply. She needn't have worried; Sarah held up the carrier bag in her hand. 'Thank you for that kind invitation, but I've just bought my supper. I treated myself to a steak. It was reduced, because it's on its use-by date, so I'll need to eat it tonight. It was a nice offer though. Maybe another time.'

Alice exhaled and said she hoped Sarah enjoyed her steak. Well, she thought somewhat ruefully as she buckled her seatbelt, I guess that answers the question as to whether this is a date or not.

*

'Have you got to know Sarah very well?' said Alice as they sped along the road heading out of town.

'Not really. I say hi to her when I see her round the place and ask her how she is. She seems pretty shy, so I don't push it.' Alice watched his hands as he guided the car into the pub carpark and dived straight into a space. He wore an elegant watch and a gold signet ring set with a small diamond on his little finger. The two almost seemed to be a matching pair. Clearly a man who liked jewellery.

They ordered their food, accompanied by small talk about the pub and the area. Once they were settled, Neil said, 'I'm sorry I haven't seen you properly since your mom's funeral, but I've been busy. I guess you know how that can be.'

'I certainly do. Back in Sydney, my job, two teenage kids, running a home on my own and trying to have a social life is challenging, shall we say.' She picked up on his light-hearted tone and matched it.

'What is your job?'

'I'm a research fellow in a biochemistry project at a university in Sydney. Not, I should add, the same one that my kids are at.'

He whistled. 'Wow. That sounds high powered. Respect!'

Alice shrugged and tried to look modest. 'I'm still on short-term research contracts, which isn't ideal. This one runs until the end of the year and then… who knows? What work do you do?'

Neil said, 'I'm an accountant. I was real lucky to land a job almost as soon as I came back from the States. I only have to go into the office once or twice a week, which suits me.' Then after a slightly awkward pause he said, 'So, how are you coping with things, Alice? I mean, it must be difficult for you handling all this on your own and being so far from home.' He studied her face with sympathy.

She was touched and surprised by his empathy. Not something you encountered that often in a man, in her experience. He even made eye contact with her when he spoke. 'It's going as well as it can. I've got an appointment with Mum's solicitor about her will, which seems pretty straightforward. And today I've made a good start on sorting out her stuff in the flat, which I was pleased about. So it's a very welcome reward to be getting out this evening.' She paused, then decided she could be honest. 'I still can't quite get my head around the way Mum died. And I keep remembering all sorts of things about her, not only from the recent years when we talked once a week and she visited me every year, but also snippets from my youth. There are things I'd have liked to ask her about, but I can't now.' Alice abruptly stopped talking. It took her by surprise that tears had risen up in her throat and threatened to engulf her.

Neil covered her hand with his on the table. The lamp caught the glint of the diamond in his signet ring. 'Tough, isn't it?' he said. 'And you're doing well handling it all.'

Alice gulped and squeezed his hand, grateful for his understanding. 'I'm so sorry. I didn't mean to get upset like that. She wiped surreptitious fingers across her eyes and attempted a smile. She remembered when he had got similarly upset in her flat.

'Your mom used to talk about you, you know. She so much looked forward to your video calls. It was easy to see how proud she was of you and her grandkids.'

'I know you used to spend time with her now and again. How did you find her? That is, how was she in those last few weeks that you knew her?' Alice realised she was still holding his hand and withdrew her own gently.

'Honestly? She seemed fine to me. In fact, I thought how lively, sociable and capable she was for a person her age. And she certainly didn't give any hint of feeling unwell or having health problems. Yup, she was a great lady, and she certainly helped me to settle in over my first few weeks here.'

Alice nodded, not trusting herself to say anything else. It was just what she'd wanted to hear, and it echoed what she had heard from various friends of her mother's.

Their first courses turned up, providing a timely distraction. The cheerful pub was surprisingly busy for a night in the week, and they both commented on this. Alice's brain was busy ruminating on how she could approach the question that was preoccupying her. Eventually she simply said, 'Neil, I've been admiring your signet ring. You obviously know and like good jewellery. Do you by any chance remember noticing my mother's engagement ring? A ring with five diamonds, quite distinctive.'

Neil frowned and looked down at his plate. He finished swallowing his mouthful of food and then said, 'I can't say I did. I'm a guy – not very good at noticing details like that. Why?' He put his next bite of seafood salad into his mouth and looked at her quizzically.

'Oh, nothing important. It's a beautiful ring, that's all. She wasn't cremated in it. I have it on now.' She extended her right hand over the table to show him.

Neil was busy with his meal, but he paused to glance at the ring.

'I expect she would have wanted you to have it,' he said. 'Do you want to try some of these prawns? They're really good.' He proffered his loaded fork to her.

Alice shook her head and thanked him. Oh well, that's another line of enquiry at a dead end, she thought. It seems he hadn't noticed Mum's ring. She decided to make an effort to put it out of her mind and enjoy the food and Neil's company.

He certainly knows how to entertain you, thought Alice some time later when they were sitting back having finished their rather elaborate but very good main courses. Neil was chatting about how this place was a 'gastropub', something which was not really a thing in many parts of the States. Alice had told him that gastropubs were starting to happen in Australia, but she didn't think she'd been to one. They got into a lively exchange about the differences between life and habits in their two adopted countries which soon fell into good-natured teasing.

'I'd recognise you as a Yank anywhere,' said Alice, indicating his plate. 'You cut your food up, then eat it with your fork in your right hand. It's a dead giveaway. Not to mention your accent, of course.'

'*My* accent? Well, the way you talk is straight out of Crocodile Dundee!' He glanced around at the other diners. 'I wonder what people are thinking about us – what are the chances of an Aussie and a Yank being together here, huh? Some sort of international experiment?'

Alice giggled. 'If you remember the heroine in Croc Dundee was American.'

He held his hands up in surrender. 'OK, I know. But you get my point.'

The waiter came by with dessert menus which they accepted and both put down on the table without looking at them.

'Oh, I nearly forgot to say, I had a message from Carrie today,' said Alice. 'You know Mum's flat? Well, Carrie asked if it would be OK for a prospective client, who's interested in renting, to come to view it. I'll reply to say I don't mind at all. So it looks like you might be having a new neighbour sooner rather than later.'

'Bit premature for Carrie to be advertising for a new renter, isn't it?'

'Not really. I've only got another two weeks left on the tenancy.'

'*Two weeks? Is that all?*' His surprise was obviously genuine. 'In that case we must get together again sooner rather than later. That is, if you would like to?'

Alice didn't need to consider her response. She'd had a nice time. And the fact that he was rather good looking and they were turning heads – well, maybe she'd imagined that– didn't hurt at all.

'This evening was just what I needed,' said Alice. 'Things are pretty full on for me at the moment, and tonight I've been able to step out of all that for a while. Thank you so much. So yes, I'd love to do it again. Maybe you'd like to come to mine and help me to finish all the food that Mum's left.'

They said their goodnights outside the Garden Flat entrance. They kissed on the cheek and Alice thanked Neil again for a lovely evening. She wondered, as she shut the door and locked it behind her, if he had been expecting to be asked in for a nightcap.

Chapter 8

'Alice Lucy Jones, where are you?'

Mum sounded cross. Alice always knew she was cross if she used all her names, rather than just Alice. She sat behind the settee, quiet as a mouse, and clutched her doll Christine to her chest. She and Christine could just get between the settee and the wall, if Alice stretched her legs out, although it was a bit of a squeeze. If she kept on growing, soon she wouldn't be able to fit, and then where would she hide? That was like the other Alice, the one who fell down the rabbit hole and went to Wonderland. She kept on eating and drinking things that made her get bigger and bigger. Then sometimes the things made her get smaller and smaller. But Alice Lucy knew that she herself would only grow bigger. That's why she had to eat up her dinner, Mum said. Even horrible cabbage.

She heard Mum going upstairs, still calling her name and asking where she was. Alice wriggled out from behind the settee, feet first, dragging Christine with her. The front room was cold, because there wasn't a fire in there during the daytime. Mum was running back downstairs now, muttering something that Alice couldn't hear. Alice stood quite still.

'There you are! Where on earth have you been?' Mum had her angry face on. 'Oh, never mind that now. We're late as it is, and we'll miss the bus if we don't leave right away. Get your coat on this minute. And put that doll down.'

Alice looked up from the photograph album open on her lap, and from the photograph that had triggered the reminiscence. She could see Frank working in the garden, lackadaisically hacking at bushes with his shears. He had cleared enough for the river to now be just visible, along with the chain link fence in front of it. As usual he wore a cap, and his loose jacket flapped with each snip that he aimed at the greenery. Alice's memory from when she was a small child of sneaking behind the settee to hide was very clear. Why did I sometimes do that, mused Alice. Perhaps it made me feel snug and safe – characteristic single-child behaviour, maybe? She also remembered that one day she must have made a noise while she was in her snug hiding place, because Mum found her and promptly dragged her out and confiscated Christine. There was no more hiding after that. Oh Mum. Alice touched the black-and-white photograph in front of her that she had just turned to. It was of her and Mum sitting on a towel on a beach somewhere. They were both wearing their swimsuits and smiling at the camera. Alice was holding her bucket and spade. Presumably Dad had taken the picture, and it was on a family holiday. Mum, if you were here now, you would have known where it was and probably what year.

People sometimes wondered if Alice had been called after the famous Alice in Wonderland, but apparently not. She had been called after Great-Aunt Alice, who was on her dad's side. Alice could only remember her as an old lady who lay propped up in bed and wheezed a lot. On the few occasions that Alice was taken to see her she had always been glad to get out of the stuffy room with its stale overlay of illness and vague grime. Their house never smelt like that – not with Mum's cleaning. Mum used to say that when she was young, Great-Aunt Alice was 'no better than she should be', a phrase that always used to puzzle Alice. In fact, it seemed that most of Dad's side of the family were a bit seedy, or 'ne'er do wells'. She thought that was the expression. She assumed that was why over the years they had more or less lost touch with Dad's side. Should I have made an effort to find them and invited them to the funeral? Alice sighed. Well, it's a bit late now. The same goes for my cousins, Uncle Tom's boys. Boys? They would be middle-aged men now, and I haven't seen them for years.

Alice wondered if she should go out to greet Frank and have the did-you-ever-see-my-mother's-diamond-ring conversation, but to be honest it seemed futile. Mum had said she used to take him a mug of tea when he was working, and he came to her last party, but that was all the contact they had, as far as Alice knew. Also, he wouldn't have been around early on a Sunday morning when she had died. So that just left Carrie and Sarah to put her questions to. Perhaps she'd get some information then. Or perhaps not.

*

'So, am I going to get a new neighbour any time soon? I've been waiting for you to tell me. C'mon, Alice – Spill!'

Neil and Alice were sprawled at each end of the sofa in Neil's flat. Empty containers, kitchen roll and glasses littered the coffee table in front of them as evidence of their very pleasant takeaway supper.

'Ah yes. The new prospective tenant for The Garden Flat. What would you say if I told you that the viewer was a blonde in her late twenties, slim and athletic, and that she's really enthusiastic about it? About as different from Mum as you could get. You never know, she might want to go running with you.'

Neil reacted predictably. He sat up in his seat. 'No way! Do you think she's going to take it?'

Alice strung him along a bit more before she admitted that she was joking. It was to his credit that he laughed about his typical male response.

The truth was that the prospective tenant certainly was different from Mum; it was a man. Carrie had brought him round to view the flat earlier that day. He had been a rather plump, quiet man, probably in his late fifties, wearing a suit and tie. Although Alice had invited him to look around freely, he had only stood in the doorway of each room to see it and hadn't wanted to touch anything or ask any questions. In fact, he had hardly shown any interest at all, so it was a surprise when he said the flat was within his budget and he would like to rent it.

After he had made the arrangements to call in at the office to complete the paperwork and had left, Carrie, ubiquitous clipboard under her arm, said 'Well, that was certainly easy. This flat seems to

76

rent itself. Your mum loved it as soon as she saw it too.'

'I can see why. It's cosy without being too small, well furnished, and with a nice view of the garden with its river at the bottom. What's not to like?' Alice straightened a cushion on the sofa, which was actually already straight from the tidy up she had given the place before the viewing. 'He seemed a bit embarrassed about looking around, don't you think? He didn't seem at all comfortable. A marriage break-up, perhaps? Oh dear. Poor man.'

Carrie shrugged and consulted her watch. 'Who knows? He's taking the flat so that's one thing less I have to do.' She hesitated, as if realising she may have been a bit tactless. 'I hope that wasn't too difficult for you, having someone look at what was your mum's last home.' Carrie reached out and touched her lightly on the arm.

'No, it was fine. I can't say I feel Mum's presence because I was never actually with her here. It's quite emotional going through her stuff, but then, that would be hard anywhere. I'm getting it done, though.' Alice recognised that this was her opportunity. 'I wanted to ask you something, if you have a moment.'

It was only for a couple of seconds that Carrie hesitated. 'OK, how can I help?' She put her clipboard and bag down on the table and gave Alice her polite attention.

Alice did her practised spiel asking if Carrie had ever noticed her mum's ring because it was missing when she was cremated, which was a bit of a mystery.

To give Carrie her due, she did give the question her attention, even though she was obviously busy. 'I can't say I ever noticed it. Lucy always looked nice, though, and wore one or two other pieces of jewellery, I noticed. Have you asked the other residents?' The short conversation went how Alice had expected.

It was later that evening that Alice finished telling Neil the story about the flat viewing and Carrie's visit. 'Yeah,' he said. 'I've noticed Carrie seems to be a busy lady. Nice, though. And I wouldn't exactly kick her out of bed.' Alice opened her mouth to reply indignantly but then realised that he was getting his own back for her teasing earlier, so she let it pass. Neil yawned and stretched his arms over his head. 'Coffee? We seem to have finished the wine.'

While Neil was in the kitchen Alice took the opportunity to stare around his living room. It wasn't too untidy, as men's places went – she had seen far worse. Apart from the standard seating arrangements and TV, the rest of the space was taken up mainly with some boxes, apparently not yet unpacked, and Neil's workstation. Alice already knew that Neil did his job mainly from home, so it wasn't surprising to see files and miscellaneous paperwork on the surface of his desk and spilling over into piles on the floor next to the waste bin. There was also a desktop computer with a large screen, plus a freestanding document holder and a lamp. He had also told her that he had started his own online business, although she was unclear exactly what that was. She had got the impression it wasn't going too well. Finally, a clothes airer stood in the corner of the room, adorned, from what Alice could see, by a towel, tee shirts, assorted socks and boxer shorts. Alice averted her eyes.

Neil put the steaming mugs down on the coffee table, along with a packet of chocolate biscuits. 'There was something else I wanted to talk to you about. I don't want to overstep the mark, but I thought I could at least run it by you.'

Alice could see that he was tentative. 'Sounds intriguing. Shoot.'

'Lucy used to provide all the outdoor plastic chairs for her parties. They're still stacked up outside, next to the door, as you know.' Alice nodded. 'She said to me once that she thought the garden could really use a bench for all the residents. Well, the obvious place for a bench to go, the only space really, would be on the patio where she… where she was found after she died. 'What do you think? Believe me, I don't mean to be insensitive. I just thought it would be a kind of memorial to her and that you yourself might like it.'

'Wow,' said Alice, 'Wow. I don't know what to say.'

'Ah, gee, I've offended you. I really didn't mean to.'

'No, no,' said Alice anxious to reassure him. 'I'm not the least bit offended. I think it's a lovely idea, especially since it was Mum herself who thought of it and wanted it. It was just… it was just a surprise, that's all. It's perfect' Alice put her hands to her face and took some deep breaths to try to subdue the emotion that had arisen within her. When she was able to look up, she saw that Neil was staring hard at the coffee table, as if he too was struggling with his feelings.

'Do you know what sort of bench Mum meant? Like, a wooden one or a metal one? I've seen plenty of wooden ones alongside the river footpath, usually with little dedication plaques on them.'

'Yeah, I've noticed them too. I think the wooden ones are more of a thing than the metal ones, don't you think?'

Alice agreed. 'I wonder if we could get a wooden bench delivered soon? I mean, it's not much more than a week until I vacate the flat and I'd like to see the bench in place before I go.'

Neil sprang up and grabbed the seat next to Alice, his phone at the ready. 'So what are we waiting for? Let's Google benches! They talked about what they thought Lucy would have liked and, after viewing several, they agreed that a traditional teak bench with a brass plaque was just the thing. Neil had moved close to Alice so that they could see the screen together. They discovered that there was no shortage of companies who supplied what they were looking for. It would just be a matter of finding one who would supply the bench quickly.

'It doesn't cost as much as I thought either,' said Alice. 'Even with the personalised plaque. Look, this company says that they supply "bespoke benches". That sounds ideal for Mum. It is sort of her memorial, after all.'

'Bespoke? I haven't heard that word since before I left the UK. In the States we would say "custom", I guess.' He hesitated, as if trying to come to a decision, then went on in a rush, 'Look, Alice, I'd really like to go halves with you to pay for this bench. This bespoke bench.'

Alice jerked her face away from the phone screen to look at him in amazement. 'What? Why on earth would you want to do that? I wouldn't hear of it!' She became conscious that their upper arms were touching while they had been poring together over the phone screen. In some confusion she adjusted her position.

'Look, I'm sorry,' he said. 'This time I really have offended you. It's just that I'll be here every day seeing the bench and sometimes using it, but you won't.'

She saw that he was distressed, and softened her own reaction, which she didn't quite understand. It was probably because she wanted the bench to be her own memorial to her mother, and hers alone. Yet it was Neil who had thought of it. 'No, you haven't offended me. It just feels like something I should be paying for. And, in general I suppose I'm always wary of men offering to buy things for me. I've got this independent streak, you see. I like to take care of myself.'

He nodded and rearranged himself to the other end of the sofa again. 'I suppose I can see that. Let's just say I misspoke. My bad.'

Alice strove to lighten the mood between them. 'I'll forgive you so long as you agree to come to me for supper tomorrow evening so that I can tell you how it's worked out with ordering the bench and when it's coming. And I thought to have just a simple plaque with Mum's name and years she was born and died, probably.

'That all sounds perfect. Shall I come round about seven?' He was smiling and looking relaxed again, so it seemed that the awkwardness had passed. He moved to the edge of his seat, so Alice took that as her cue to leave.

Alice gasped when she looked at her watch. 'Oh my, it's nearly eleven!' I had no idea it was so late. I'm sorry if I've stayed too long. You've got work first thing tomorrow.'

Neil got up so that he could show her out. 'Of course you haven't stayed too long. I like talking about your mom and I like your company, Alice.' Suddenly he was serious. 'I think you're the nicest person I've met since I've been back in the UK. And it's ironic that you're not even British.'

Alice giggled as he slid his arms around her in a hug. This time he kissed her gently on the mouth. Then he released her and opened the door. As Alice stepped out, she thought she heard the door close upstairs at Sarah's flat. But she wasn't sure.

*

It was just after breakfast the next morning when there was a knock at the door. Alice got up to answer it and managed to keep the smile on her face when she saw it was Jane and not Neil. Jane was holding Charlie's hand, and they were both sheltering under a gigantic umbrella against the rain, that was falling steadily.

Despite wanting to get on with ordering the bench, Alice knew that she had to invite them in straightaway out of the rain. They exchanged the expected remarks about the change in the weather, and Alice offered coffee.

Jane declined, and said, 'I don't want to keep you long, because I expect you've got lots to do. It's your last few days here, isn't it?'

Alice said it was and led Jane to sit in the living room, since she could hardly keep them both standing in the small hallway. Charlie had scampered ahead of them.

'Lucy used to live here, didn't she, but she's dead now so she's not coming back.' He looked around at the room which was now stripped of its ornaments and paraphernalia. 'Do you live here now?' he said to Alice.

'No, I'm only staying here for a bit and then I'm going home, back to where I really live.' Alice had squatted down so that she was on his level. She contemplated explaining who she was and where she lived, then decided it wasn't really necessary. He regarded her seriously, like children do. 'Lucy used to give me biscuits,' he said.

'Charlie!' Jane scolded him gently. 'That's not very polite.'

'It's OK,' said Alice, getting up from her squatting position. 'I'm really sorry, Charlie, I don't have any biscuits or anything like that.' She put her a mournful expression on her face. She hadn't seen much of Charlie, but from what she had seen he seemed to be a nice little boy. And Mum had liked him, apparently, and even looked after him sometimes. 'No school today, then?'

Jane answered for him. 'It's an INSET day.' Seeing Alice's blank expression, she added, 'An In-Service Training day for the teachers, so school's not open for the kids. I've managed to arrange my shifts around it.'

'So how can I help you?' said Alice.

'Ah yes. The ring of your mother's that you mentioned had gone missing. Did it ever turn up?'

'No...' Alice felt herself cringe as she continued the lie.

'Well, Lesley and I were talking yesterday, and Lesley suddenly remembered that early on the morning of the day when your mother died, Frank's van was parked outside. I expect you've met our gardener and odd job man? He works for the property next door as well as us. We didn't actually see him here when we were outside and dealing with the situation, but anyway, I thought you might like to know he was around then. He might have seen something unusual.'

Chapter 9

It had been a busy day, so Alice felt justified in having a glass of wine early. This time next week I'll probably be heading home, she thought. Back to my normal life. This strange interlude, full of emotion, memories and sadness will be left behind. Although the grief and the knowledge that I'm not going to see Mum again will stay with me. I guess once I'm back home I won't have all the admin of Mum's affairs and clearing of her possessions to distract me. Then I will be able to process my grief and let it normalise.

And as for this ring business, I'm totally sick of it. Alice sighed as she started to replay the last two conversations in her head. By afternoon the rain had stopped and when she had been coming back from the shop, laden with bits and pieces for the evening, she saw that Frank's van was outside The Beeches' drive. Therefore, now would be just the time to catch Frank and talk to him, following Jane's extra bit of information this morning. So she had approached Frank bearing a mug of tea. He was grateful and seemed pleasant enough in his manner. They spoke of the overnight rain and Frank said that he was glad of it because it meant he didn't have to water the garden. He was quite chatty, in fact, and openly told Alice that he was gardener and handyman for several houses hereabouts and that the extra pin money on top of his pension was very welcome.

'It's impressed me how well looked after The Beeches is,' said Alice. 'And the residents all seem very nice. I think it's a grand place to be living, and I know Mum was very happy here.'

Frank drained his mug noisily. 'Yes, she's missed, is your mother. But when it's your time to go, better to go quickly than to linger, is what I always say.'

Alice agreed and followed his remark. 'And I believe you were around here on the very morning that she died.' Did he look a bit startled, or was she imagining it?

'Was I? I can't say as I remember. My head's getting like a sieve lately.'

'Oh… it's only that someone said your van was outside, and it seemed awfully early to be around on a Sunday.'

'Ah yes, I remember now. They were having a bit of trouble next door with a leak, so I had to call round. I didn't come into here, though.' He kicked at a stone with the toe of his boot. 'I'm glad I didn't. She would have been lying here…' He stopped, perhaps realising he was being insensitive.

Evidently he hadn't been at The Beeches that morning. Or so he said. Alice pressed on. 'Frank, I know you didn't see my mother often, but did you ever notice a lovely diamond engagement ring she used to wear?'

Frank shook his head. 'Can't say I did. I bought my wife, God rest her soul, a ring with a diamond in when we got engaged. It was a real beauty, just like her, and she loved it. I've still got it in the house. I never noticed your mother's though.'

Alice pressed on feeling that her interrogations were increasingly futile. 'The ring went missing, and Mum wasn't cremated in it. I just wondered if you might have seen anything that pointed to how she lost it, that's all. And I'm sorry about you wife, Frank.'

So her conversation with Frank had ended up being another useless enquiry. Alice took another sip of wine and looked at her watch. Neil was five minutes late. Surely he wasn't going to stand her up? That would not be a good end to her day. So she was very relieved to hear the knock on the door a couple of minutes later and to see him standing there. His hair was wet which made it appear darker and more tousled than Alice had seen it before. At first, she wondered if it was raining again but when he stepped in and brushed her cheek with a kiss she found he smelled of soap and shampoo, so presumably had just stepped from the shower.

'Sorry to be running a bit late. I fitted in a run with a friend after I'd finished work and well, time just got away from me. You know how it is.' He handed her the bottle of wine he had brought.

Alice took up his blithe tone. 'No worries. It's only a cold supper anyway that I just picked up from Tesco Express, because I've packed away most of Mum's cooking utensils. A charity is going to collect them in a couple of days' time.' She thanked him for the wine and went to get glasses.

When she came back, he had made himself comfortable on the sofa. Tonight he had teamed his jeans with a plain blue shirt which was left open by a couple of buttons at the neck and a pair of crocs on his bare feet. He seemed to be able to carry off both stylish and casual at the same time, and she liked that in a man.

'You know the million-dollar question,' said Neil. 'How's the great bench project progressing?'

'Done and dusted, I think,' said Alice with some satisfaction. 'I've ordered a nice one from a local company, which I thought might speed up delivery, and they've told me they can fulfil the order in a couple of days. Perfect!'

'Fantastic! I guess, formally, you should just run it by Carrie, but that shouldn't be a problem. She'll love the idea.'

'Oh, I hadn't thought of that. But I'm sure you're right, nobody will object.'

'And the plaque?'

'I went with keeping it simple. Just her name and year of birth and death.'

Neil nodded. 'Classic. I'll think of Lucy when I sit on it. And I'll think of you.'

Alice got up in some confusion. 'I've laid the food out on the table in the kitchen. Shall we eat? I daresay you're hungry after your exercise. It's only salads, cold meats and stuff. I hope that's OK.' She realised she was babbling.

For a time, they talked about Neil's day, although he claimed that accountancy was so boring that no-one would want to hear about it. He told her more about his run after work and how he had completed several marathons while he was living in the States and was thinking of a doing a marathon here next year, if he figured he could find the time to fit in the training.

'Back home I'm into running too,' said Alice. 'But I packed so quickly I didn't end up bringing the proper training shoes with me. Which is a shame, because a run would have been a good stress management tool.'

'Yeah, it sure is that. We could have run together, you know. That would have been great.'

She met his eyes. 'Maybe. But you would have been faster than me. It wouldn't have worked.'

'I'm sure we could have made it work.' He was teasing her with his smile. Then he changed the subject. 'Anyway, what have you been doing today, apart from chasing up the bench?'

What has occupied me a lot today, thought Alice, is that cursed puzzle of the ring. She had called to see Sarah which, not surprisingly, had turned out to be no more successful than her conversation with Frank. Sarah had answered the door after Alice had knocked a second time. She opened the door a few inches, then seeing who her caller was, opened the door a bit further but remained in the doorway, blocking Alice's view inside, always supposing she wanted to see it. She was wearing a knee-length grey skirt and a patterned blouse. Very teacherly garb in Alice's opinion.

After they had greeted each other, Alice realised she that wasn't going to be asked inside so she plunged in with her question. 'Sorry to bother you like this, but I guessed you might be at home since it's an INSET day.'

Alice's attempts at showing off her knowledge backfired because Sarah said 'It wasn't an INSET day at my school. But as it happens, I got home quite early today. Is there something I can help you with?'

Not exactly openly hostile, but not exactly friendly either, was how Alice would have described the reception at Sarah's front door. So without further preliminaries Alice got on with it and asked the standard questions that felt as if she could now recite them in her sleep. Sarah shook her head and said she had never noticed this ring and knew nothing about what might have happened to it. There seemed no reason to prolong the awkward exchange, so Alice thanked her and left.

As Alice was heading down the stairs, Sarah called after her 'I saw you leaving Neil's flat last night. Quite late.'

Alice paused on the stair, then thought that there was nothing she wanted to reply to that remark.

She decided not to tell Neil about her encounter with their neighbour upstairs, and by the time they were sat at the kitchen table with their supermarket supper, they were talking like old friends.

Neil helped himself to more quiche. 'I guess you're looking forward to going home, right?'

'Yes… Yet I have to say it has been quite an eyeopener being here. I've felt like I've got to know Mum more by seeing where she lived and meeting her neighbours and some of her friends. That's really helped me to absorb the shock of her death. But yes, of course… I'm looking forward to seeing the kids, especially.'

'It's two kids you've got, and they're both in university, didn't you say? And their dad is an Aussie?'

'That's right. I was working in Sydney for six months on a placement when I met Dan. What can I say? He swept me off my feet with his raw masculine charm, I got a permanent job, we were married three months later, and I never went back to Britain, except for my dad's funeral. A fairytale romance.' Alice realised she hadn't been entirely successful in keeping the bitterness out of her voice. 'Mum and Dad came over for the wedding and to be fair, once they could see I was dead set on doing this thing, they accepted it with a good grace.'

'But it went wrong, huh?'

Alice sighed. 'Not until a while after Zoe and then Joe were born. By then the cracks were starting to show and so when Dan had an affair that was serious, well… that was it. But by this time Sydney had become my home, and the kids had been born there, so there was no question of me living in another place. And I wanted the kids to still be near their dad.'

'And you haven't met anyone else? A lovely woman like you?'

He's flirting with me, thought Alice. Just be cool. 'There have been boyfriends over the years, but nobody special. What about you? Did you leave anyone special behind?' She met his eyes, more boldly than she would have done if she hadn't just drunk more than half a bottle of wine.

'Nah,' he said. 'If you want the truth, I'd just got out of a bad break-up, which is why I came back to the UK. Diana found someone she preferred and dumped me. As simple as.' He shrugged. 'I'd thought I'd probably come back to my roots sometime. I just didn't think it would be yet.'

'Well, we're a right pair of lonely hearts, said Alice with an attempt to lift the mood. 'Tell you what, let's go into the living room and have some brandy. I can't take it with me on the plane, so we might as well.'

They had to drink the brandy out of tumblers, because Alice had already consigned the brandy glasses to the charity shop. They both sipped at the warming spirit, and Alice wondered whether to bring up what was niggling her. She put her glass down on the coffee table to stop herself from drinking it too fast. 'Neil, could I talk to you about something? You see, I could really do with having a sounding-board about something.'

He matched her actions and put his glass down. 'Shoot,' he said. 'I'm intrigued.'

Alice signalled to him to wait a minute while she went into the bedroom. 'It's about Mum's ring. Do you remember I asked you if you had noticed it and said that she wasn't cremated in it?' She showed him the ring, which she had fetched from the bedroom and put on her finger. He nodded, looking puzzled. 'Well… it's a crazy story, but I feel I have to tell someone, or I'll go mad.' She took a gulp of her brandy and coughed as the spirit hit the back of her throat.

'You see, the first I knew of the ring's whereabouts was the day after the funeral when it was anonymously posted through my door in a little envelope. No note, no nothing.'

Neil had crossed one foot over his knee, and his foot had been gently bobbing up and down. He stopped. 'What? Are you sure it's the same ring?'

'I'm sure. I grew up with that ring. It was promised to me when I got engaged except that everything happened too quickly for that. Besides which, why would any person want to put anything through my door without telling me?' As she had expected, Neil was at a loss. 'First of all, I checked with the funeral directors, of course, but they had never seen the ring. Then, I've asked everyone who lives at The Beeches, or who might have taken it, or knew something. But I've drawn a total blank.' Alice couldn't keep her exasperation out of her voice.

'What did they all say?'

'Jane and Lesley denied knowing anything about the ring. I thought they might have seen it since they discovered Mum and were first on the scene. Although Jane did make a point of calling on me the other day to give me some potentially useful information – she had seen Frank's van here on that same morning. The morning Mum died, that is. I talked with Frank, but he didn't know anything and was quite uninterested, to be honest. The same with Carrie and with Sarah. And you'd already told me that you hadn't seen it. So it's a complete mystery. Oh, but wait a minute – didn't Sarah just buy a car? I supposed she had saved enough money or had a windfall or something, but…'

'Aren't you forgetting? The ring was returned to you.'

'Oh yes. You're right, it doesn't make any sense.'

Alice covered her face with her hands and groaned. 'Oh, it's so exasperating.' She dropped her hands back into her lap. 'Well, thank you for listening. It feels a bit better to have got it off my chest. It was just going round and round in my head and driving me insane.'

'At least now you have the ring back, and you can treasure it to remind you of your mom. It looks great on you, by the way.'

Alice held her right hand out and contemplated it as she moved her fingers so that the light from the lamp made the stones glitter. 'It certainly is a beautiful piece.'

'So now it's back in your family. Your very own family heirloom. Look, Alice, I get it that this whole thing is weird, but you'll be able to let go of it and forget all about it when you get home.'

Alice felt his common sense and kindness like a hug. She sat back in her chair and allowed herself to relax. 'The Jones family heirloom, indeed. I wonder if Zoe will want it when she gets married? Not that her name is Jones, of course, but it was my name before I got married'

'How old is Zoe? Cool name, by the way.'

'She's nineteen, a year older than Joe. She was born when I was twenty-five, a year after we got married. She's quite a way off from thinking about marriage, I hope. Just for her to be getting through uni is enough to be going on with. Her and Joe are both good kids, but they're teenagers, and you know what that's like.' Then she added in some embarrassment, 'Sorry, I forgot you don't have kids.'

'It's OK. You know, Diana and I never talked about getting married and starting a family, even though we had dated for more than a year. She was always sort of elusive. In the last couple of months that we were together she seemed even more distant, and she changed the subject if I tried to talk about the future. But I never imagined there was someone else. It seems obvious now, looking back.' He swallowed the last of his brandy in one gulp.

Alice reached out and laid her hand on his. 'I'm so sorry. It must have been really tough for you.'

Neil curled his fingers round hers and shook his head agitatedly. 'Gee, I'm sorry. What an idiot I am! You don't need to hear about that, with your mom hardly cold and all this ring stuff you've been dealing with. Diana and I are over now anyway, and I've moved on.'

'No worries. You've helped me by listening to my ring story and reminding me that I can put it behind me when I go home, so it's only fair if you offload onto me too.' Alice was about to offer him another drink, but he seemed to gather himself together and stood up. 'I should be going. I hope I didn't stay too long.'

'Of course not.' Alice got up to be the good hostess and see him out. Then on impulse she added, 'We'll see each other again before I go, won't we? I haven't booked my flight yet, but I've got to be out of here before the end of the month.'

'I'd be sad if we didn't.' He held her gently by the shoulders and kissed her mouth. 'I'd like to see you every day while I still can. But now I should go.'

'We should be able to arrange that,' said Alice, trying to sound nonchalant, and not as flustered as she felt. She opened the door for him. 'Now, should you sneak out, or should we make some noise to give our neighbour upstairs something to ponder?'

After they had finished sniggering as silently as they could, they decided that it would be courteous for Neil to go quietly to his door, because it was late.

Alice went back inside, collected the empty glasses from the living room and took them to the kitchen. She contemplated the debris of their supper and decided to leave the clearing up until the next day. It was time for bed. She went into the bedroom, where she had turned the bedside lamp on earlier in the evening. She ran her hand over the bedlinen, smooth and faintly fragrant because she had changed it earlier that day.

Chapter 10

Lucy lay in bed blinking at the ceiling in the rather frowsty motel room. There was a background hum that she couldn't identify. The little fridge, which they hadn't put anything in yet? Maybe. Or perhaps it was the traffic outside? Or the air conditioning unit? No, they hadn't turned it on last night because it was April, so they didn't think they'd need it. Although, when they had staggered in from the airport yesterday with their cases, disoriented and dishevelled from the long journey from London to Sydney, it had seemed pretty hot. Lucy found it hard to think that here April was the start of autumn rather than the start of spring.

Kevin was lying next to her on his back, snoring gently. It seemed a shame to wake him since he was obviously deeply asleep, but she knew they had better make a start to their day and try to adapt to Sydney time as soon as possible. Plus, Alice was picking them up for lunch. She had driven to meet them yesterday at the airport, but she had been really sorry that she had commitments for the rest of the day, so she would have to leave them to settle in at the motel on their own.

'Kevin, love…' Lucy stroked Kevin's face. She thought how the signs of middle age were more evident when he was sleeping – wrinkles that pulled his mouth down and sagging skin round his eyes. It must be the same for me, thought Lucy. At least women would be likely to do something about the grey in their hair. She'd had her roots done the day before they flew out. 'Kevin', she repeated, more loudly this time, and changed the stroking to gentle prodding. He grunted and moved away from her fingers but didn't open his eyes. 'Come on, love, it's nine o'clock.'

'Would that be morning or evening?' The words seemed to dribble from his mouth.

'I know what you mean.' Lucy got out of bed and opened the curtains. You could almost convince yourself that they were still in the UK, given that the traffic drove on the same side of the road here. 'I'm going to put the kettle on, and then I'll have a shower. She pulled the tea bags out of their luggage – they always brought their own from home – and plopped one in each of the mugs.

By the time she came back from the shower, Kevin was sitting up in bed sipping from his mug and scratching his belly. 'What did you think of Alice yesterday? Did she seem strange to you?'

Lucy was concentrating on fastening her bra. She put her arms through the straps and wriggled her breasts comfortably into place before she replied. 'I suppose she did seem a bit distracted. But it's only four more days to the wedding, so it's not surprising she's a bit stressed.'

'Well, I'm glad we travelled out here when we did and not any closer to the actual day. Give us a chance to get rid of this bloody jet lag. I've always hated it.'

Lucy was rummaging through one of the suitcases. Although she had hung up Kevin's suit and her mother-of-the-bride outfit yesterday, the rest of their clothes were still unpacked. She paused in her search. 'What do you mean, 'always'? It's only the third time we've done this trip.' She pulled out two summery dresses and held them up for inspection. 'To tell the truth,' she continued, 'to me it's exciting, even though the long journey is a bit tiring. At least you get smiling flight attendants bringing you food and drink all the time and you don't have to clear up. And you get to watch films.'

Kevin grunted. 'I suppose. I just feel like shit now, that's all.'

She didn't add that he didn't look his best, either. 'You'll feel better when you've had a shower and got some breakfast inside you. I'm trying to decide which of these dresses would be more suitable. I want to look nice when we meet our future son-in-law for the first time. I was thinking the orange one with the short sleeves, but I don't want to look too over the top. What do you think?'

'You know it's no good asking me.' He swung his legs out of bed and sat on the side while he stretched his arms over his head, making his shoulder muscles ripple. 'You always look nice as far as I'm concerned. You always have.'

Still not an ounce of fat on him, thought Lucy. 'That's lovely to hear,' she said. She put the dresses down and squeezed round in the cramped room to come and sit on the bed next to him in her underwear. She kissed him on the cheek, and he put his arm round her. 'Just think – in four days' time you'll be walking our daughter down the aisle. Well, so to speak. I don't think they have an 'aisle' as such in a registry office.'

'To be honest I'd feel easier in my mind if we'd met this Dan beforehand. And if it wasn't so rushed. She's only known him for less than half a year. Which isn't a lot, as knowing goes.'

'I know. I'd hoped for something different too. But what can we do? Alice is old enough to know her own mind. And she seems so settled in Australia.' Lucy resolutely pushed her own qualms to the back of her mind while she could still stop herself putting her own misgivings into words. She stood up briskly. 'Anyway, we're here now so let's make the best of it. You'd better start hurrying and get in that bathroom to freshen yourself up before we see Alice. And her fiancé.'

*

On the morning of Alice's wedding, Lucy knocked tentatively on Alice's hotel room door. She strained to hear any sounds coming from inside the room, but all seemed to be quiet, so that probably meant Alice's invitation for a wedding morning breakfast was for her alone. Good. Lucy wanted to connect with her daughter one-to-one for a time before the whole wedding day pandemonium kicked in. But really, Lucy corrected herself, there wasn't going to be much possibility for pandemonium because of the stripped-down-ness of the proceedings. Just a handful of guests in the registry office, the standard legal requirement declarations to the celebrant, Kevin playing a notional role as father of the bride, Alice's best friend and Dan's brother as witnesses. Afterwards, they were going to have lunch in the hotel where the principal wedding guests were now staying. A minimalist wedding.

Before going to sleep last night, Lucy had reminisced about her own wedding. There were about seventy guests, as she remembered. Her parents had stumped up for the whole thing, as was common in those days. She had walked sedately down the aisle on Dad's arm, her classic white dress generously cut so as to mask any slight thickening around her waist. The rushed nature of the event due to Lucy's pregnancy had been tactfully played down. Most of the guests wouldn't have known for sure, although most could have made a good guess. Even after all these years she could still conjure up the excitement that coursed through her as she made her way towards the man she loved, to join her life with his. Kevin had turned around to look at her, his beloved cheeky grin all over his face.

The reception had been a jolly affair, not posh (because they weren't posh or wealthy) but full of love and happiness. After the ceremony she had put her engagement ring on top of her brand-new wedding ring, which enhanced the beauty of both, she thought. After the wedding breakfast there were the usual speeches. Lucy couldn't remember quite what was said, but she was sure they were just plain and simple expressions of good luck and the joy of the day. Then she had changed into her going-away outfit and they had left for their honeymoon on the coast, to the accompaniment of clattering cans tied to the back of the car. That was a thing back then.

Just then a memory jumped into Lucy's mind. As she and Kevin were leaving the wedding reception, a black cat had crossed their path – a traditional sign of good luck. We've got photographs with that cat, thought Lucy. She looked across to where Kevin was sleeping peacefully on his side of the bed, his chest rising and falling sedately with his breathing. We have had far more good luck than bad, thought Lucy. We have stayed close and still have a lot of fun together. We both have jobs and a nice home. Perhaps the only real bad luck has been not being able to have any more children after Alice. The melancholy that she still sometimes felt threatened vaguely. But we have had Alice, and she's always been a blessing, even though she lives on the other side of the world now and isn't having the wedding I'd always imagined for her, thought Lucy. Stop it, she's living the life she's chosen. Lucy had turned over and resolutely closed her eyes to go to sleep.

At her hotel room, Alice, in her dressing gown with her hair bundled into a thick hotel towel, answered the door to Lucy's knock. They hugged enthusiastically as Lucy stepped in. 'Today's the day,' said Lucy, her face next to Alice's cheek. Her neck smelled of good quality soap.

'I can hardly believe that by lunchtime I'll be a married woman.' Lucy could feel her radiating excitement. 'We're doing it the traditional way, Mum. Dan and I are not going to see each other this morning before we meet at the registry office.' She took off her towel turban and fluffed up her damp locks of hair. 'And of course Dad's going to walk me in to give me away.'

Lucy kept her smile in place and thought how there wasn't much else that was traditional about this wedding. No bridesmaids, no proper reception with speeches, apparently. Would Alice be wearing the long white dress that Lucy had hoped for? She doubted it. 'Let's see the dress, then.' She kept her tone light to match Alice's excitement.

The outfit was nice enough. The fabric was a light green background, with darker green polka dots. It was knee length and had a matching bolero-style jacket, where the fabric had been reversed – a dark green background with light green polka dots. Alice held it on the hanger, up against her body, swinging round so that Lucy could appreciate the swirliness of the skirt. 'Do you like it?' said Alice. 'I designed it and had it made especially.' She examined herself in the full-length mirror.

There was only one right answer and Lucy gamely gave it. 'Oh, what a stunning creation! You're going to look fabulous in that! Are you having any flowers or anything in your hair to finish it off?'

Alice was just shaking her head and saying that she was keeping it simple when there was a knock on the door. Breakfast had arrived. A trolley bearing a fresh fruit platter, a basket of pastries, sparkling wine on ice, orange juice and a pot of coffee was wheeled in. 'Wow, I'm being spoiled,' said Lucy as Alice mixed the wine and orange juice together. Apparently, that was called a mimosa. She raised her glass in a toast to the forthcoming wedding. They clinked glasses and tucked into the breakfast. This is just like old times, thought Lucy, as they chatted away, increasingly easily. How pleased I am to see my darling girl so happy.

'I'm so glad that Dad and you had a chance to meet Dan before the wedding. What did you think of him?' said Alice.

Lucy didn't have to fake this one. 'I thought he seemed a very genuine young man, and he obviously thinks the world of you.' She chose not to add that the whole business of them getting married seemed a bit rushed and they might have benefitted from getting to know each other for a few more months before they took the plunge. Besides which, it was all decided now, and Alice was a grown woman, capable of making her own decisions. She had pointed this out to Kevin, when he had been rather less approving about Dan. But probably no man would be good enough for his daughter.

They laughed and chatted their way through breakfast, getting quite nostalgic over memories of Alice's childhood. When they were replete with mimosas and food, Lucy broached what she had been building up to ever since Alice had opened the door to her. 'Alice,' she said, suddenly formal, 'I've got something to say. You've known well enough since you were a little child that I was given this diamond ring by my future mother-in-law when your dad and I got engaged. It had been passed down to her by her mother.' Lucy held her hand out and, with a flourish, withdrew the ring from her finger. She proffered it to Alice. 'And now, following the family tradition, it's yours. With love and blessings from your dad and me.'

Lucy had seen this moment in her imagination. Alice would exclaim and reverently place the ring on her finger with joy. But it wasn't quite like that. 'Oh,' said Alice, obviously nonplussed and making no move to take the ring. 'Your ring, Mum. Your diamond ring. I'd forgotten all about that. But surely you don't want to part with it, do you?'

'I'd like you to have it. You don't seem to have an engagement ring, and it is a family heirloom. You know it was always intended that it should be passed on to you.'

Still Alice made no move to take the ring. She laughed nervously. 'The thing is, I'm having a very wide wedding band, so there wouldn't be room on my finger for a second ring. And, if I had been going to have an engagement ring, I think Dan would have wanted to have bought it for me himself.' She reached out and laid her hand on Lucy's arm. 'Oh Mum, I'm sorry. It's a lovely kind offer and I'm touched. It's just not quite right for me, that's all. Please don't be disappointed.'

Lucy replaced the ring on her finger with as much dignity as she could muster. 'If that's what you want. Only I thought…' She saw Alice's puckered face and made a huge effort to get herself under control. There was no way she wanted to fall out with her daughter on her wedding day. 'Look at the time, and you haven't even started doing your nails or your hair yet! Can I help?'

Kevin and Lucy sat on the front row in the register office while the wedding of Dan and Alice was solemnized. There were some twenty other people in the room, including Dan's parents, several of his relatives, and a few friends. Alice did indeed look very elegant in her green outfit. Lucy watched the tall, good-looking couple making their declarations in front of the registrar. Tears crept down her cheeks. But that was alright – it was a wedding. You were supposed to cry.

*

It was in the last box of Lucy's photographs that Alice found the pictures of her wedding that Dad had snapped, getting on for twenty years ago now. Most of the photos she was going to consign to the trash, but just a small number she would take back home with her. For instance, there was this one with her and Mum together, both with a glass of champagne in their hand and beaming at Dad's camera. They were holding hands, and their heads were tilted towards each other. Alice could just see the gleam of her new wedding ring. Whatever had possessed me to have that wide wedding band, she thought. It was totally impractical, making my finger get sore underneath it all the time. And I let it be the main reason why I didn't accept Mum's engagement ring when she offered it to me.

She recalled the wedding day breakfast that she had she shared with Mum. With critical honesty she let herself remember how she had dismissed Mum's heartfelt gift. Although she realised that time could distort memories, she knew this one was brutally accurate, as knowing goes. I turned the ring down flat, even though I knew well enough it was a precious family heirloom with an associated tradition. How can I have hurt Mum like that?

She contemplated the ring where it now rested on the finger of her right hand. If I had accepted the ring from Mum back then, all this exasperating situation that's happening now would have been avoided. It's my fault. She jerked the ring from her finger onto the table, and it bounced off onto the floor. I hate it, she thought. It's bad luck, even cursed, maybe. Then she bent to pick the ring up from where it had landed under the table. She knew exactly what she was going to do with it.

Chapter 11

Alice wandered round to the front of The Beeches, trying to calm her thoughts, her phone still in her hands. It was shaping up to be a lovely summer morning, not too hot but with the sky settling to a pale crystalline blue. What she had planned to do this morning was to book her flight to take her home and then head into town. But now the phone call she had just taken threw everything into confusion.

'Hi Alice, I haven't seen you for a few days,' said a voice behind her. 'I thought you might have left already.' It was Jane, with Charlie holding on to her hand and swinging round on it. In her other hand Jane held a little backpack. It was red, with Charlie's name emblazoned on it.

'No… no, not quite yet. I have to be out of the Garden Flat by the end of the month.' It seemed rude not to stop and chat, even if it was the last thing that Alice wanted to do at the moment. 'Hi, Charlie. I like your backpack. I wish I had one like that.'

'It wouldn't fit you. You're big like Jane.'

'Well, that's true,' said Alice, feeling lame because she couldn't think of another answer right then.

'We're just off to the childminder's,' said Jane, car keys in her hand.

'Ah yes, it's school holidays now, isn't it. Well, I won't keep you.'

'Can I give you a lift anywhere?'

'Thank you, but no. I'd just wandered outside to see… to see how warm it was.'

'OK.' Jane paused. 'Is everything alright?'

Alice always got the impression that Jane could assess her with a glance, that she could see straight into her mind. She pulled herself together. 'Yes... yes of course. Well, I've done my weather assessment now. It's definitely a T-shirt day. Have a nice day, Jane. Have fun with the other kids, Charlie.'

Jane pulled a face. 'Work for me, I'm afraid. Come and say goodbye to us before you leave, won't you.'

Alice assured her that she would. She walked back to her door and listened to the sound of Jane's car leaving. She still hesitated before she knocked on Neil's door. It was gratifying that his face lit up when he answered the door and saw it was her, even if there was a fractional pause before he invited her in.

'I'm so sorry – I know you're working, but are you free for a few minutes?'

'I've got a meeting online at ten, but I've got a few minutes. What's up?'

Alice told him. 'I had a phone call this morning from the company who's supplying the bench. They're really sorry, but they have some issues which mean that they won't be able to deliver the bench until next week. I don't know what to do. I've got to be out of the flat before that! They said they'd give me a small refund for my inconvenience, but that doesn't help in the circumstances. Shit, shit, *shit*!'

'Hey, it's OK, it's OK.' Neil took her in his arms. 'We'll figure something out.' Neil was only wearing a pair of shorts, so whereas his hug was soothing, it was also distracting. Alice indulged in it until Neil gently led her to the sofa and sat her down.

'I was about to book my flight back home,' said Alice, holding on to his hands. 'It's just as well that I didn't. Oh, everything was going to fit in so perfectly, time-wise. I've all but finished clearing Mum's things, then I just had to take delivery of the bench to finish things off. But now this! It seems crazy that I've coped with it all, the funeral arrangements, the admin and stuff, but this has just floored me.'

Neil put his arms around her again and stroked her face. 'Shh...' he said as if he was comforting a child. Alice felt herself begin to calm down. She put her hand on his naked chest. His heartbeat was steady under her palm and gave her the anchor that she needed.

'I'm sorry,' she said, 'I just lost it there for a minute.' She sat up and gave him a weak smile, trying not to let her eyes drop to his torso. 'It's just that… well, I don't know what to do now.'

'There is an obvious solution,' said Neil, his voice calm. 'I can take delivery of the bench. I'll take plenty of pictures and send them to you. I'll even take a selfie so you know what it looks like with a person on it.'

Alice shook her head. 'I really appreciate that offer, and you trying to cheer me up, but I need to see the bench in place for myself. You see, Mum didn't have a grave, so this is all the memorial there will be for her. And it's particularly poignant that the bench will be put at the place where she died.'

Neil reached and gently squeezed her hand. 'Yeah, I get it.'

Alice sighed and ran her hands over her face. 'I'm sorry to have come bursting in on you like this with my problems, especially since you have a meeting coming up in a few minutes. I guess I'll just have to go into a hotel for a week, that's all. It won't be so bad.'

'That's one solution,' said Neil. He got up and walked to stare out of the French windows, his back to her.

'What else can I do?' Alice was puzzled.

He came back to the sofa and sat on the edge of it. 'You could stay here.'

'Here? But I have to be out by the end of the month because there's another tenant ready…'

'No, *here*. In this flat. With me.' He was serious now.

'Oh… you mean *with* you?'

'I have a perfectly serviceable double bed. Would you like to see it, Alice?' He was smiling again now as he teased her.

Alice floundered for her words. 'Oh, what a shock… I don't know what to say…'

His picked her hand up and kissed it, slipping his tongue lightly between her fingers.

'I think you know exactly what to say.' He stood up, pulling her up with him. 'There's nothing I would like better than to show you that double bed right now, but it's only…' he consulted his phone, 'five minutes until my meeting starts. It's an important client so I can't be late.' His eyes travelled from her face down to her body. 'I can't even kiss you now because I wouldn't be able to stop. But you'll come round this evening?'

'Yes,' was all Alice could think of to say.

Neil dived into the bedroom and came out carrying a shirt and a tie, which he quickly put on. He tucked the shirt into his shorts.

'Aren't you going to put some trousers on?' said Alice.

'Nope. It's way too hot, and anyway no-one will see me below the chest.'

Alice gaped at the incongruous combination of the smart shirt and scruffy shorts. Then she couldn't help it, she just guffawed noisily. She was still laughing when Neil bundled her out of the door, and she staggered back to the Garden Flat.

*

There were several jewellers with well-known brand names around the town centre, having showcase windows sparkling with every kind of ring – engagements rings, signet rings, wedding rings, friendship rings. They were made from gold, silver, and other metals, and studded with diamonds, emeralds, rubies, sapphires, as well a whole host of semi-precious stones. If I had decided to have an engagement ring, I wouldn't have a clue how I would have chosen from this lot, thought Alice as she gazed, almost hypnotised, at sumptuous arrays of gems displayed enticingly before her. Expensive jewels and adornments have never really been my thing, if I'm honest, she thought. I've got a few pretty trinkets, such as my abalone shell earrings and my opal pendant, but I can't call anything else to mind that I'm fond of. All the more reason for doing this today.

The jeweller's shop that Alice eventually settled on was buried in a lane off the main street in town. It wasn't the sort of shop that would usually draw the eye; it was dark and cave-like, with a small frontage and only a modest selection of bangles, necklaces, rings and earrings in the window. What attracted Alice was that in smaller letters under the name, Branson and Son, was written 'Family jewellers since 1927.' Somehow that chimed with her mission today. Of course, first she had cleared it with Zoe. She had phoned her late yesterday evening, which was morning in Sydney.

'Mum? What's up?' Alice could hear female voices and the clatter of crockery in the background, which she took to be breakfast in Zoe's student accommodation.

'Hi, Zoe. First of all, there's nothing wrong. But I need to run something by you, fairly urgently seeing as how I'm coming home soon.'

'Oh, right. Only I don't have long because I have to leave for a lecture soon. Can't you message me?' Alice could hear the subdued impatience in her voice.

Alice realised too late that she could have messaged her, but then Zoe might have taken her time replying. Anyway, she was talking to her now, so she pressed on as succinctly as she could. 'Do you remember that beautiful diamond engagement ring of Granny's? By family tradition it's supposed to be passed down to you, but I was thinking of selling it instead and splitting the money between you and Joe. What do you think?' Alice couldn't begin to explain to her how she now was repelled by the ring and couldn't wait to get rid of it.

'Is that it? Sell it, keep it, give it away, I don't care what you do with it. I don't want it anyway.'

Well, that was pretty unequivocal, thought Alice. 'Thanks, Zoe. I just needed to check with you. Are you OK?' Alice could hear someone calling to Zoe that they were ready to go.

'Yes, I'm fine, but I've really got to go.' But then she hesitated a minute. 'Is everything OK with you, Mum? Only you sound a bit, sort of, weird.'

Alice took a breath. 'Everything's good. It's just that there's a lot I've got to pack in before I come home, that's why I sound a bit flustered. No worries. You get off now, and I'll message you later.'

An old-fashioned bell clanged as Alice opened the door to the shop. A young woman, not much more than a teenager, pushed open a heavy curtain and came out from the back of the shop. As the curtain fell back Alice caught a glimpse of a wooden workbench cluttered with various tools and paraphernalia.

'Hello,' said Alice, 'I was just wondering… you have some second-hand items for sale in your window, and I have an antique ring I'd like to sell, and I wondered if you'd consider taking it, please?' Alice wasn't quite sure why she was nervous.

'Have you got the ring with you?' Alice produced it and the girl picked it up to inspect it closely, pushing back her long hair behind her ears, revealing several piercings. 'It's very pretty,' she said.

'Yes… yes, it's been in my family for some generations.'

The girl laid the ring back down on the counter. 'I'm afraid my father isn't here to value it at the moment. You're very welcome to leave it with us and he can take a look at it.' When Alice hesitated, she added, 'Of course, I'll put it in the safe and give you a receipt. Or you can come back when he is here.'

'Oh.' Alice was nonplussed. Somehow, she had had the image of leaving the shop with a fistful of banknotes and the ring out of her life for ever, but perhaps that had been unrealistic. 'When will your father next be here?'

'He may be back this afternoon, but I'm not certain. He should definitely be here tomorrow, though.'

The ring sat between them on the counter, looking increasingly malevolent to Alice. Having made a decisive step toward getting rid of it, she felt distinctly reluctant to take it back with her again.

'Do you have any shopping to do or something, and maybe he'll be back then?' The girl was obviously trying to be as helpful as she could. Perhaps she was unused to having the whole responsibility of the shop to herself.

'No, I can't wait this afternoon.' The anticipation that she was keeping firmly in control flared up inside her. After this I need to get back to The Beeches to have a shower and shave my armpits before my date this evening, she thought. And now it certainly was a date. 'I will leave the ring here in your safe, please, and I'll come back tomorrow afternoon, if that's OK.'

She watched while the girl tagged the ring and carefully locked it in the safe. Then she wrote out the receipt and handed it to Alice.

'The shop is called Branson and Son, but shouldn't it really be Branson and Daughter, since you're obviously part of the family business?' said Alice.

'Ah, the name refers to my father and my grandfather. Grandad opened the shop in 1927. There's a picture up there on the wall of how the shop looked back then.' She pointed to a grainy black and white photograph in an ornate frame. A man in a suit and waistcoat stood proudly outside the door, and the sign across the frontage said 'Branson's jewellers. The outside of the shop had changed remarkably little, and you could recognise it as being the very same one that they were in now. Alice said as much to the assistant.

'I know. We're very proud of the traditional feel we maintain in Branson's. It sets us apart from the high street retail chains.'

'So, it's your father who is the jeweller here now?'

'That's right. He took over the business from grandad a couple of decades ago. Grandad still looks in about once a week, though, to keep his hand in.'

'And you? Have you followed in the family business?' Alice found herself fascinated by this little enterprise, which had endured unspoiled all these years.

'Me? Oh no. I just help out now and again, usually when Dad has to go somewhere.'

The door chime clanged again, and another customer came in. Alice thanked the jewellery girl for her help, said she would be back tomorrow afternoon, and tucked the receipt for the ring safely in her purse.

She gave one last look back over her shoulder at the little shop as she headed to the main street. Bottle of wine, she thought. I must pick one up to take to Neil's this evening. This evening… she caught her breath as she thought about it. Was it wise? Probably not. But it had been a long time since she had encountered a man who attracted her as much as Neil. She wondered what Zoe would have said if she had casually mentioned her plans for the evening.

*

They weren't finding much to say to each other, but then, perhaps they had said it all without words. Neil's hand was on Alice's naked thigh as she lay curled against him, their bodies breathing together, and the duvet discarded somewhere on the floor. Alice watched the evening sunshine reach its fingers across the bedroom ceiling. She was hardly aware of what she saw, but the shadows were pleasant and seemed to echo the serenity that bathed her.

Suddenly Neil whipped his hand off her leg. 'Aw shit! I didn't shut the drapes!' He sprang out of bed and yanked the curtains belatedly across the window. He came back to the bed and stood laughing down at Alice. 'I guess we were in too much of a hurry to notice before,' he said. The curtains were thin, and Alice could still easily make out his shape. It was the first time she had had the chance to see his entire naked body, since the time from when she arrived at Neil's flat to when they had landed on the bed had been about two minutes. She liked what she saw.

Alice put her hand across her mouth to catch her giggles. 'You mean anyone who happened to be strolling on the patio could have looked in and seen us? It could have been Sarah! Oh my…'

Neil lay back down on the bed on his side and propped himself up on his elbow. 'Let me look at you,' he said, his eyes tracing the same path that his hand was taking. 'You're beautiful, you know.'

Alice didn't think her body had ever been called beautiful before. It was a pretty standard body, she felt, but his words made her glow, and she felt uncharacteristically at ease with his scrutiny. She opened like a flower to his gaze and touch.

It was getting quite dark in the bedroom when Neil said, 'I had a vague idea of us ordering takeout when you came round this evening, but that doesn't seem to have happened. But I'm quite hungry now. How about you?'

'It must be all the energy you've expended,' said Alice. 'I can't

107

say I feel especially hungry, but I guess we'd better eat. Don't bother with ordering food – let's have whatever you've got in your kitchen.'

'I'm a guy, remember. I don't think we're going to find a whole lot in there.' He put on his boxers and left it at that. Alice grabbed his T-shirt and pulled it over her head. It was infused with the smell of his body, and she inhaled deeply.

They raided the fridge and cupboards and managed to come up with some elderly bread, eggs, and a tin of baked beans. When they were sat at the table with their supper, Neil said between mouthfuls, 'Oh yeah, I remember now. I want to talk to you about the bench. I had a thought.'

'Mmm?' said Alice, her mouth full of egg. She had found she was hungry after all.

'After it's been delivered and put in place, how about getting everyone into the garden to see it and have a drink, as a sort of, I don't know, memorial to your mom?'

'Oh… you mean a little ceremony, to dedicate the bench?'

'Well, I wasn't thinking as formal as an actual ceremony, more just a get-together, a bit like your mom used to organise. We all appreciated them you know. Unless you want a ceremony, of course? You call the shots here Alice.'

Alice thought about it. 'You know, that's a good idea. It's especially poignant since the bench is going to go where she actually finished her life.' She saw Neil wince. 'That was really thoughtful. Thank you.'

Neil reached over and touched a tendril of her hair between his fingers. 'I was fond of Lucy. As I told you, she reminded me of my own mom, and she was kind to me while I was settling in. Hey, what do you think she would say if she knew what had just happened between us?'

'How could she be anything else but delighted when she saw how happy it's made me?' said Alice. They leaned across the table and kissed, the baked bean flavour in their mouths mingling.

Alice brought them back to the topic in hand. 'So yes, I think the bench thing could work. But the question is when? It will have to be soon.' She couldn't bring herself to say she would have to leave shortly after the bench arrived, but they both knew it.

109

Chapter 12

Alice looked again at the words she'd typed on her phone:

Hi all, sorry it's been some time since I've been in touch. Things are all but wound up here, and I plan to be back in work next Monday. Thanks for your patience and good wishes throughout my absence. Let's have a meeting, probably next Monday afternoon, when you can catch me up on everything. Best regards, Alice.

She re-read the email and then sent it. It felt distinctly odd to her after all that had happened recently. She had hardly given her work life a thought. However, she knew the four postgrads who comprised her research group would be glad to get her message. It wasn't fair to leave them dangling any longer, without her supervision and not knowing when she was coming back. In other circumstances when she went away, for example to a meeting or symposium, she kept up fairly regular contact with individuals in the group and always had her finger on the pulse of what was happening. But not this time. The strange thing was, whereas normally she liked her job and was quite engrossed by it, this time she wasn't looking forward to returning and taking up the reins again. It seemed like a place she no longer inhabited, something she had grown out of. It was strange and she felt disorientated. Alice frowned as she looked out at the garden.

There was only an internal wall between her and the room where Neil was working in his flat. She got up from her chair and went to lay her hand and then her cheek against the wall that separated them. Would he hear me if I knocked on it, she wondered. She raised her fist to try it but then dropped it again. She knew he had meetings, and she really shouldn't disturb him. It was Monday, and he had to return to the reality of a working week.

The weekend that they had just spent together had been incredible. Unbelievable, in fact. For Alice, it was as if some magic portal into a new existence had opened for her. She knew that sounded corny, but it was exactly how she felt. She and Neil had both lived in a state of bliss for the last two days. When they had been temporarily sated by sex, they had talked for hours, either sprawled on Neil's bed (with the curtains closed this time) or, when they needed fresh air and food, walking by the river or sitting in a country pub holding hands. They didn't seem to run out of things to say to each other. Neil had shared details and anecdotes of his years in New York, Alice traded with tales about the life she had established in Australia. They even ventured into talking about their previous partners and break-ups. Alice thought that was easier for her than Neil because she and Dan had divorced many years ago, whereas Neil's ending to his relationship with Diana was still relatively fresh. She also learned that Neil had nearly been married when he was younger. They had grown apart and eventually separated fairly amicably. It was after that he had decided to take his chances on a new adventure and move to America.

They talked about everything but the future.

Alice wandered round her mother's flat, trying to harness her scattered thoughts and emotions in order to think rationally about what was happening to her. How could she feel so elated in the wake of Mum's death? Yet she felt sure that Mum would have approved. After several years of bad dates and relationships that didn't quite go anywhere, she had earned this. She could just hear Mum saying: this romance might not be for very long, but you deserve a bit of fun and to know that not all men are a waste of space. You take it for what it is and enjoy it, my girl.

But Alice couldn't let herself dwell on thoughts of Mum, or indeed anything else, because Carrie would be here soon. Alice took one last look around the flat. The work surfaces were bare, the bed stripped and the kitchen utensils in order. She had emptied the rubbish and cleaned the bathroom. Mum would have been proud of her.

The doorbell rang. Carrie was right on time and looking as smart and professional as she always did in a neat jacket and tailored trousers. Alice held the door open for her, and they exchanged their hellos.

'Well, this is it,' said Carrie. 'It only seems like five minutes since you arrived. Although, I'm sure it doesn't seem like that to you.' As she spoke, she was looking round the flat appraisingly.

'I'm not sure what it seems like. It's been such a rollercoaster journey,' said Alice.

Carrie nodded, cursorily inspecting each room. 'I have to say you're leaving the property in tip-top condition. The cleaner won't have that much to do when she comes in tomorrow.'

'I'm grateful that you allowed me to stay here, Carrie. It's made things so much easier, and it gave me some closure to be in Mum's last home.'

Carrie's reply was muffled, because her head was in the hall cupboard so she could note the electricity meter reading. She emerged, patting her hair back into place. 'I think that's just about it. All I need now is your key, and there's a couple of places for you to sign.'

When the last tasks were duly completed, Carrie said, 'Frank and I are really grateful for the invitation for a drink tomorrow evening. To dedicate Lucy's bench, as it were. I think it's a lovely idea to put a memorial for her right there in the garden.' She craned her head to look out of the window. 'I see the bench has been delivered. It fills the space there just right. In fact, it looks like it's always been there.'

Alice followed Carrie's gaze out of the window to where the brand-new bench stood. 'Yes, I'm very pleased with it. The company just delivered it this morning. Thank you for giving permission to have it there, Carrie.'

'Oh, not at all. Now, what would you like us to bring? Some snacks?'

Alice shook her head. 'No, thanks. Bring a bottle if you like, but it's not going to be a garden party like I believe Mum used to host. I was thinking just a drink or two and a few nibbles.'

'Gotcha. We'll be there, anyway and will raise a glass to Lucy. By the way, which hotel are you going to now? I don't see your luggage. Have you checked in already?'

So here it was. Alice had thought that as a courtesy, since she represented the landlord, Carrie would have to know she, Alice, was staying in Neil's flat. She hadn't known quite how to raise the topic. She decided that the direct approach was best, so she said, 'Actually, I've been staying with Neil since Friday.' Rarely had Alice seen a person look more dumbfounded. She continued steadily, 'I'll be there until I go home, which is only a few more days.' When Carrie didn't reply she added, 'So I'm just a very temporary guest with Neil, of course.'

Alice kept her gaze level and non-confrontational, she hoped. Carrie's thought processes were transparent. First, she was totally taken by surprise, then she decoded what it was that Alice was implying. As the truth dawned, a slow grin spread over her face. 'Do you have the expression in Australia, "You're a dark horse?"'

Alice recoiled from Carrie's salacious expression. 'Yes, we do,' she answered stiffly.

'Well, I would never have guessed. You and Neil!' Carrie was obviously enjoying herself hugely. 'I bet it's done you the world of good, having a bit of a fling, after all the sadness and trouble you've had.'

A fling? Is that what this is? thought Alice.

'Do the other residents know?' said Carrie. 'We've never had anything like this this here before. At least, not that I've known about.' She all but winked at Alice.

'I have no idea,' said Alice, trying to supress the memory of the open curtains when they had made love for the first time.

Carrie seemed to be totally oblivious of how uncomfortable she was making Alice. 'He's certainly a good-looking guy.' She leaned in closer to Alice and dropped her voice confidentially. 'So tell me, what's he like, then?'

Alice turned away abruptly. 'I'm sorry to rush you Carrie, but I've got some errands to run in town, so I really must get on.'

*

Luckily Alice paused long enough when she opened the door to his flat to hear that Neil was speaking, so she was able to close the door quietly and creep in. He was talking to three people on screen, and he was wearing the shirt, tie and shorts that had so amused her the first time she had seen them. He put out a hand to wave to her while he continued his conversation. Alice silently made her way to the kitchen and closed the door. She drew a glass of water from the tap and sat down at the table to drink it. Her breathing was gradually returning to normal as she tried to calm down from her mortification at Carrie's response.

A few minutes later Neil burst in noisily. 'Hey, gorgeous,' he said. 'Are you now officially homeless? Wanna hang out with me?' He opened the fridge, pulled out a carton of milk and took a mighty swig. Alice couldn't help but smile. Carrie was right; he was a fine-looking bloke. He leaned over and gave her a smacking milky kiss.

'You're cheerful.'

'Well, I've just had a successful meeting and there's a pretty girl in my flat who I think I just might get lucky with later.'

'We'll have to see about that, won't we.' Alice pulled him towards her by his tie, and they kissed again.

Neil enquired how it had gone with Carrie. 'Was she cool with you staying here?'

'Yes… Well, yes.'

'You don't sound too sure. What's up?'

Alice tried to get her thoughts in line. 'Nothing, really. It's just that she thought it was sort of… titillating. The idea of me staying here with you, that is.'

Neil pushed his chair back and roared with laughter. 'No way! Oh, that's great! What did she say exactly?'

'She actually asked me what you were like. There was no doubt about what she meant.' Alice struggled to maintain her dignity. 'At that point I said I had tasks to do and showed her out.'

'What d'you know! If that doesn't just take the cake! Didn't you want to let on just a little something about me? I know how you girls talk.'

Neil's amusement and masculine reaction about the Carrie conversation was not at all what Alice wanted to hear at that moment. She folded her arms. 'You're treating this like a huge joke. I know it plays to your male vanity, but to me it was mortifying.'

Seeing that she really was offended, Neil quickly came around the table and tried to make amends by putting his arms around her. 'Hey, I'm sorry, babe,' he said into her hair. 'It just quite funny, that's all'.

His breath was warm on her neck, and she savoured the endearment which he hadn't used to her before. 'Well… it was just a total surprise. And Neil, there was something else she said…'

'What, babe?'

'She said it was "a fling". Is it a fling, you and I?' He didn't respond straightaway, and Alice held her breath while she waited for his answer.

'No, I wouldn't call it a fling. Short duration, sure, but I think we both know it's a bit more than a fling.' His voice was serious now.

He released her and they stood gazing at each other. 'I wish I wasn't going home on Friday,' said Alice.

He fingered a lock of her hair. 'You don't really mean that. There's your kids and your job to get back to.'

Alice didn't know what to say. Eventually she came up with, 'Why does life have to be so complicated sometimes?'

Before Neil could reply, his phone rang. He looked at the screen. 'I have to take this – it's my boss.'

Alice took the opportunity to calm her feelings while Neil was in conversation so that when he turned back to her after his short phone call, she was able to present an unsteady smile.

'I'm sorry, but there's some work I must finish off today, since I'm taking tomorrow off,' said Neil. 'And we have to be ready for the garden party tomorrow evening. Seven o'clock, isn't it?'

'That's right. But there's hardly any prep to do. I've got the drinks and nibbles, and Lesley and Jane are providing the glasses and a table to put stuff on.' She saw his eyes drift towards his workstation, and she took the hint. 'I have a couple of things to get in town, so I'll leave you to get on with your work.'

He drew her to him and kissed her gently, in his trademark way. Then he said, 'And we're going to have a day out tomorrow! It's going to be just great. I'm so looking forward to a trip to the beach with you.'

'Me too,' Alice replied. 'A special day out.'

'I'm looking forward to seeing you in your swimsuit.' He let his eyes rove over her body.

Alice gasped and put her hands up to her face in dismay. 'Oh no, I didn't bring my cossie with me!'

Neil guffawed. 'Cossie? Is that what you guys say down under?'

'It's a perfectly normal word as far as I'm concerned.' Alice tried to maintain her dignity. 'But what shall I do? I didn't exactly think of a cossie, that is swimwear, when I was packing to come here.'

'Hmm. Stopping to get one on the way might take a while, and we have to be back for early evening.' Neil thought for a minute. 'I know, why don't you ask if you can borrow one off the girls upstairs? They look about your size. Or Sarah, of course.'

'I can't imagine Sarah having any swimwear, let alone lending it to me. But Lesley or Jane… that might work. I'll pop round later.' Alice thought again. 'But no, what am I thinking? Nobody wants to lend something that intimate to someone else, especially someone they hardly know.' She put on her best smile and grabbed Neil's hands. 'Could we just stop at a mall on the way, and could you let me run in and get something? I'll be ever so quick. Honestly.'

Neil allowed himself to be persuaded, stipulating that Alice's purchase had to be a sexy bikini. Alice judiciously changed the subject. 'Neil, have you seen the bench? It was delivered this morning and it looks really splendid. I hope they didn't disturb your work call while they were delivering it.' Neil told her he hadn't seen it yet, so he opened the French doors, and they both stepped out onto the patio to view the new addition to the garden. The sturdy wooden bench was a pleasant mid-brown hue which Alice thought harmonised perfectly with the summer abundance of the garden. It would look equally as good with a dusting of snow in the wintertime. The memorial plaque to Lucy was simple and not too overt, which was just how Alice had imagined it.

'Wow,' said Neil, almost reverently as they stood assessing it. He reached out and stroked the wood. 'What a totally perfect memorial to Lucy. I'm glad I knew her, even if it wasn't for very long.' Neither of them moved to sit on the bench.

They went back into Neil's flat and stood quietly with their arms around each other, both allowing their own thoughts. Eventually Alice said, 'You really should finish what work you have to do today, then you can take me for our day out tomorrow with a clear conscience.' She reluctantly disentangled herself from his embrace and walked towards the door.

'Alice…'

She turned back to him, her bag dangling from her shoulder. She thought anew how utterly beguiling he was with his lazy smile and his dark wavy hair. Not to mention his slim muscular body.

'We've just got these few precious days left to us. Let's make the most of them and have some fun.'

'I couldn't agree more.' Alice blew him a kiss and left.

*

'Do take a seat while you're waiting and I'll be with you soon.' The man behind the counter at Branson and Son Jewellers indicated the chair in the corner of the little shop, next to the cabinet displaying bracelets, necklaces, earrings and other trinkets. He was busy attending to a young couple who were poring over a tray of rings. Alice didn't mind waiting. It was best to be out of Neil's flat so that he could get on with his work undisturbed.

From the snatches of conversation that she could hear from the three people at the counter, it became obvious that the couple were looking for an engagement ring. They were both young, in their twenties perhaps, and dressed similarly in jeans and T-shirts. In fact, they might have been brother and sister, judging from their appearance and slim build, but of course they weren't. There was one ring that the girl seemed to favour and, after picking it up to examine it, she slid it onto her finger.

She held her hand out to admire the effect and seemed pleased with what she saw. Her boyfriend was also nodding enthusiastically. Alice heard the word 'sapphire' mentioned, so she presumed that was the principal stone that the chosen ring featured. After some nodding of heads, the man got his credit card out and paid for the ring, which was put into a box and then a bag. Alice speculated that perhaps there would be a party or a family meal to celebrate the occasion of their engagement. She smiled and offered them her congratulations as they left the shop, hand in hand. Her heart warmed to the happy young couple when she thought of them going forward to their shared life together. She wondered if, should Mum's ring already have become part of the pre-loved, antique ring selection in the shop, they would have chosen it. The recipients of Mum's ring were not destined to be that particular couple, because they had happily settled on the sapphire, but no doubt some other lovers in the near future would choose her diamond ring. Mum would have been happy about that.

While Alice had been waiting in the shop she had also ruminated on why she had kept quiet to Neil about her mission today. She concluded that she hadn't told Neil that she was selling Mum's ring mainly because events had overtaken them. In other words, they had just spent the whole weekend in a haze of lust and, if she was honest, they had had better things to concern themselves with than that goddamn ring. In fact, she had clean forgotten that she had said she would come back the next day, after the jeweller had valued the ring, to collect the proceeds of the sale. Such was the magical state she had been in over the weekend that it had totally gone out of her head. She would tell the jeweller she hadn't returned the next day because something had come up. Which was true.

But there was an additional reason lurking at the back of her mind why she hadn't told Neil about the prospective sale. After all, she'd had plenty of opportunity to tell him today where she was going, and she had chosen not to. Why? Really, she knew perfectly well why. It was because he might have tried to talk her out of it, and in truth she just wanted to have done with the whole thing. She acknowledged to herself that this was not least because of associated uncomfortable memories of when she had rejected the ring. She didn't like to think of how she had brushed it aside when Mum had tried to give it to her, as part of a family tradition, on her wedding day. That must have hurt Mum. Alice was ashamed, and she didn't want to go into that whole thing with Neil.

'I'm sorry to have kept you waiting. What can I do for you?' The jeweller was a genial middle-aged man with a pleasant manner that seemed to fit the shop ambience to a T. He briskly polished the glass-topped counter as he spoke to her.

Alice explained her errand and muttered her apologies that she hadn't returned on Saturday, when she said she would, to complete the sale. She was clutching the chit she had received as proof of her ownership of the ring, ready to hand over to the jeweller, who she presumed was Mr. Branson.

The man adjusted his glasses and scrutinised the receipt. 'Ah, yes,' he said and disappeared into the back of the shop. 'Just a moment.'

Alice was puzzled. She hoped this delay didn't mean that they weren't able to take her ring as part of their second-hand collection. Mr Branson returned with a small, labelled bag and tipped the ring out onto the counter.

'I'm very sorry Mrs...' he read her name off the label, 'Mrs Smith. We won't be able to take your ring.'

'Oh,' said Alice, not able to hide the disappointment from her voice. 'I was led to believe that you'd definitely be wanting to buy it. It is a lovely diamond ring, which has been in my family for generations.'

'If the piece actually had been set with diamonds we would have been very keen to purchase it. But you see, Mrs. Smith, these stones are not diamonds. I'm afraid the ring is a fake. I'm very sorry.'

Chapter 13

It would take about two hours to drive to the coast, so Neil had told her. They had set off in the early morning before the heat of what promised to be a lovely summer's day had got going. On the way they had stopped off at an out-of-town shopping outlet and without wasting too much time drank coffee in Starbucks. Then Alice had dived into a Marks and Spencer's to pick up a swimsuit, or a 'cossie' as she liked to continue to call it, just to tease Neil. She had insisted on going alone to make her purchase because she felt that Neil's ideas and hers of what might be appropriate beachwear for a woman her age might not be the same. In fact, she ended up buying two swimsuits, on the grounds that they would take up hardly any room in her luggage, and it had been a long time since she had bought a new cossie.

'Hey, you were quick,' said Neil from the driving seat, as she jumped into the car with her purchases in a bag. 'C'mon then, show me!' He tried to grab the bag, but she moved it out of his way.

'No way! I'll model it when we get to the beach, and you can see it then. Now let's get going, because we can't waste too much time if we're going to be back in plenty of time for the bench thing.' One of the swimsuits that Alice had bought was blue and plain, a proper 'swimming costume,' for proper swimming, and the other one, which was the one she intended to wear, was a classically-cut, strappy one-piece in a tropical print. Neil only protested half-heartedly that she wasn't going to show him, and in no time they were on the motorway and streaming south towards the coast.

Alice sat back and relaxed while Neil drove. He drove quite fast, so the miles were soon eaten up. His driving struck her as skilful and confident, and she let her eyes travel over his bare forearms as with relaxed hands he guided the air-conditioned car past lorries and other slower moving traffic. The hairs on his arms were dark and masculine looking, the same as his legs. However, she couldn't see his legs very well while he was driving, so she feasted her eyes on his arms.

Neil broke into her daydream by saying, 'I've been thinking about that stuff you told me about your mom's ring. You know, about it being worthless.'

'Oh, yes?' said Alice. After Neil had finished work yesterday, she had briefly recounted to him how she had taken the ring to be sold so that she could split the proceeds between Joe and Zoe, and then how taken aback she had been to learn that the diamonds were fake, so essentially the ring was worthless. Neil's total surprise at this turn of events had almost matched her own. However, she hadn't wanted to discuss it very much. The whole business of the ring was now distasteful to her. And anyway, she didn't want one of their remaining precious evenings hijacked by spending time talking about it.

'You told me that the story passed down through the generations was that your great-grandfather or whoever it was stole the ring off of a gypsy, right?' When Alice assented, Neil continued, 'Well, surely, it's unlikely that a gypsy would have a trinket made of diamonds as part of their wares? So it kinda makes sense that the thing is a fake.' Neil indicated left for the slip road to exit the motorway.

'I suppose you're right,' said Alice after a moment. 'I'd never thought about it, I just took it for granted. It was part of our family folklore, right from when I was a little girl, and I just accepted it without question, like Mum and Dad seemed to.' The memory flashed into her mind of how, whenever Mum or Dad had again told her the tale of the pretty lady and the ring, she was required to solemnly recite the mantra that really stealing is naughty, and she mustn't do it. And it seemed that the example had stuck, because never in her life had she stolen anything.

The car swung off onto a side road. 'Are we nearly there already?'

said Alice, glad to leave the vexed topic of the ring behind. When they arrived at the car park, they had to join a queue of cars that was starting to form there, and they agreed it was just as well that they hadn't left it until later to set off. They parked the car amongst rows of others, many of them disgorging families toting paraphernalia such as backpacks, beach toys, parasols, cool boxes and inflatables. Various kids tagged along in sunhats and flip-flops. Alice and Neil were travelling light in comparison: Alice had a shoulder bag to carry her personal stuff, water bottle and swimwear, whereas Neil only had their two towels and his swimming trunks under his arm. A feeling of freedom and being untrammelled grew inside her.

They claimed an area of pale smooth sand that was within easy sight and sound of the lapping waves. Alice wrapped her towel around her to change modestly into her new swimsuit. Neil approved with a loud wolf whistle that attracted the amused attention of their beach neighbours. Alice covered herself with sun cream, even persuaded Neil to use a bit, donned her sunglasses and lay back in the sunshine. She felt Neil reach for her hand, and they allowed the warm sand to trickle through their joined fingers. Only three more days, thought Alice. Two and a half if you count the journey to the airport. How is it possible to feel like this in such a short time? Thoughts of her home, her job and even her kids seemed insubstantial. Home was just a suburban house that she wasn't particularly attached to, her job contract was up for an uncertain renewal at the end of this year, and this left Zoe and Joe. They were wrapped up in their own lives nowadays and perfectly happy to communicate sporadically with their mum via messaging and the odd phone call.

'Come on, said Neil, suddenly jerking her fingers and sitting up. 'Let's do it.' He jumped up and dragged her with him. They asked the nice family next to them to keep an eye on Alice's bag and jogged down to the shore. The water was deliciously refreshing after the heat of the sun, and they waded in, allowing the cool water to gradually claim their bodies. Out of the corner of her eye Alice watched Neil splashing water on his chest. Then he dived under the hump of the next wave and resurfaced with a great splash, like an exuberant sea creature. Alice gradually immersed herself more decorously and, with her head out of the water to keep her hair dry, breast-stroked gracefully out to join him. They swam out to sea and, treading water, turned to see the miniaturised people on the beach. They swam back and frolicked around like a pair of kids and then strolled hand in hand along the shoreline to let the sun and the gentle breeze dry their bodies.

Lunch involved queueing for hot dogs and chips (or French fries as Neil called them) from the van, then sitting cross-legged on their towels to eat them.

'It's been years since I had a hot dog,' said Alice, licking yellow mustard from her fingers.

'You don't say? It's standard fare for a New Yorker. Classic street food. Can't beat it.'

'Isn't there a song about "going to Coney and eating baloney on a roll"?' Not that I know what baloney is.'

'Ah, baloney. That's a kind of sausage, which we usually eat cold. And Coney is Coney Island, a beach resort which was about half an hour from me, if the traffic was OK.'

Alice bit into a chip. 'Yes, I've heard of it. What's it like?'

'Crowded. And not what you would call sophisticated, what with all the razzamatazz. But I guess you could say it's fun. I've only been a couple of times. It's not exactly my scene. In Sydney you've got Bondi Beach, right?'

'Yes, we have. It's not the only beach, but it's the most well-known. About six kilometres south of Bondi is Coogee beach, which is where we go. You can walk between the two beaches if you want. It takes about an hour.' Her mind flashed back over the barbies she had had over the years on the beach, including ones with Mum when she had been visiting. She firmly cut the reminiscences off, not allowing herself to become too nostalgic. 'I remember one year,' she said, laughing, 'when there was a heatwave. The temperature was in the high thirties. I was in the sea at Coogee beach, literally just standing there with the water up to my neck, virtually shoulder to shoulder with crowds of other people. It was a best way to try and keep cool.'

'That doesn't sound like much fun.' Neil finished the last of the meal and wiped his hands on the towel. 'Do you miss Coogee beach and your home?'

'Not really. I'm surprised by how much I *don't* miss it.' She opened her arms to indicate their present vista. 'What could be better than this? And this is without the searing temperatures of a Sydney summer, that can spoil it. How about you? Do you miss New York?' She waited for his reply with some trepidation, although she wasn't quite sure why.

They had also bought two iced coffees from the fast-food van, and Neil was taking the lid off his. 'No, I can't say that I miss New York,' he said after he'd taken a slurp of his drink. 'I never really had plans to settle there for ever. The Big Apple's not really the kind of place that you want to make your permanent home. Unless you were born there, I guess. When I was going out with Diana… well, then I thought about staying. But then we broke up and coming back to Britain became a no-brainer.'

'And are you glad you did? Come back to Britain, that is.'

'Oh, sure. I've got a job I can handle, some buddies, a nice flat in a nice town. And then I met a lovely woman. The thing is, she lives on the other side of the world.'

Alice kept it light. 'But right now, she's not on the other side of the world, she's right by your side. Assuming you meant me, that is.'

Neil put his arm around Alice. They sat quietly and gazed at the people-dotted sea for a while. Ask me to stay, she thought, just ask me. Yet she knew she wouldn't be able to say yes. Not now, anyway. But perhaps later when my contract is ended… She didn't dare to examine that idea too closely.

Neil said, 'I was just pondering our two cities, at least my ex-city, and how they both have quite famous beaches, which we've both visited. And here we are now, between those two places, on another beach. Not a well-known beach this time, but it seems like… seems like…' he groped for his words. 'It seems fitting for us to come together in the middle, right here, right now. At least something like that. I'm not very good at this sort of crap,' he finished awkwardly.

'Wow. That's very profound. I hadn't taken you for a

philosopher. I think I get what you mean. What were the odds of two people from two different continents encountering each other like this on another continent and…' Alice had nearly said, 'and falling in love', but she stopped herself. 'The beaches seem like a metaphor for our story.'

'Now who's being all deep and thoughtful? OK, you win.' Neil decisively finished his coffee and looked at the time on his phone. 'Babe, we should be heading back. There's an important gathering this evening, and you are the hostess.'

'You're right. We have to shower the salt off our bodies, and I must shampoo my hair.' She leaned over and whispered in his ear.'

'Sex in the shower? Boy, you are a naughty girl! So we'd definitely better hurry.'

The tide was starting to go out.

*

Over the last month Alice had got used to not drying her hair. Mum hadn't possessed a hairdryer, and neither did Neil. That Neil didn't have one was no real surprise, because he was a man, but she was mildly curious that Mum hadn't seemed to own a hairdryer. So, Alice had made do with allowing her hair to dry naturally and cultivating the tousled look. She quite liked it.

She had vigorously towelled her hair, squirted on some leave-in conditioner and combed it through with her fingers while it was still damp. She moved to the bedroom and pulled on fresh jeans and a pretty blouse. She peered into the mirror to fix her necklace in place and roll on a bit of lip gloss. With her summer tan, her face didn't need any make-up. She smiled at her reflection. Did that look like the face of a woman who had had sex less than half an hour ago?

Alice went through the French doors to the patio, where Neil was arranging the small table and a few chairs. She carried with her a bowl of potato crisps and another of corn chips. Then she went back for a couple of bottles of wine and some juices and beers.

'I think it's all hunky-dory, once the girls turn up with the glasses,' said Neil. He looked around the scene approvingly. 'The

Lucy bench is definitely the focal point, which is perfect.'

'I'm so grateful to you for helping with all this, Neil. It was even your idea to get the bench in the first place.'

Neil shrugged. 'You're very welcome. I told you; I really liked Lucy. She was caring and sweet. And she'd got her finger on the pulse alright. She never seemed as old as she really was.' He paused, then went on briskly, 'They'll be showing up soon. How do you feel? Nervous?'

'No, not really,' said Alice. Then with more honesty, 'Well, a bit. I'm going to say a few words, and I hope I can manage it without getting all choked up. I'm used to speaking in front of people at seminars and meetings of course, but this different.'

'Gotcha. Have a glass of wine before you start. That'll do it. And you already know that everybody's real friendly. It's not like they're strangers.'

Alice said, 'Oh, by the way, talking of strangers, I put a note through the door of Mum's flat – I should call it the Garden Flat now – inviting the new man, who's called Carl, to drop by for a drink. I forgot to mention it to you.'

'Good idea. Since the guy's my neighbour now, I might as well get to know him.'

There was a flash of colour across the patio. It turned out to be a toy car pushed by Charlie. He chased after it and stopped short when he saw it had gone under the new bench.

'Hi, pal. It's OK, you can get your car. Will you show it to me?' said Neil, crouching down to Charlie's level. He held the little car out for Neil's inspection, and the two entered into a male-bonding dialogue about the car. It occurred to Alice that Charlie probably didn't get a whole lot of contact with men.

Following Charlie were Lesley and Jane, carrying the promised glassware. They had included wine glasses and a few tumblers, and they unloaded them onto the table. Alice exchanged helloes and kisses with them. 'Only a few days until you go home,' said Lesley. 'Are you all set?'

'I will be by the time I get on the plane,' was Alice's enigmatic reply.

Both Lesley and Jane simultaneously glanced towards Neil, where he was still engaged in earnest conversation with Charlie. So it seemed that Carrie had told them. Jane said, 'It's great that you and Neil have become an item. Do you plan to keep in touch?' Lesley beamed encouragingly.

Their total absence of judgement was refreshing after Carrie's reaction. Alice said, 'I'm sure we'll stay in touch. But there's no real plan.' She was saved from having to add any more by the arrival of a man who she didn't recognise. He stood uncertainly on the edge of the patio.

Alice went up to him and held out her hand. 'Hello, I'm guessing you must be Carl. I'm Alice. My mother was the tenant in the Garden Flat before you took it over. I know you didn't know my mother, but I thought you might like the chance to come along and meet everyone. I've found them to be really friendly.' Carl took her hand momentarily and muttered "pleased to meet you", after which he didn't seem inclined to say anything. He was a middle-aged man, dressed quite formally in trousers, a plain white shirt and a muted tie, and he seemed rather overwhelmed by the occasion. Alice served him with his choice of drink, which was orange juice. Then she said, 'Let me introduce you to some other residents at The Beeches. She led him to the group which comprised Lesley, Jane and Neil, all holding glasses of wine now and chatting with ease. Charlie was sitting on the bench waggling his feet and lower legs, which were sticking out over the edge of the seat. Once the handshaking with Carl was underway, she was able to leave them to it and go to greet Carrie and Frank, who were just arriving. Carrie was looking as smart as ever in white trousers teamed with a dark blue top, giving a saucy nautical look, whereas Frank maintained his usual slightly seedy demeanour.

'Alice!' said Carrie. 'How are you?' She indicated the bench, which Charlie had now vacated in order to raid the bowl of crisps. 'Doesn't your bench look absolutely splendid, right there. Don't you think it looks splendid, Frank? Thank you so much for buying it for The Beeches. It was a fantastic gesture.'

Alice wondered if Carrie's over-effusiveness stemmed from her realisation that she had overstepped the mark with her comments and probing about Neil last time they had met. Well, whatever. It scarcely mattered now. 'Yes, I'm very pleased with it. Perhaps I'll see it again sometime.' Did she imagine it or did Carrie's smile sag briefly?

Frank had been standing rather awkwardly, and now he said, 'It's a grand thing that you've done, alright. Lucy would have been pleased with the way it just sets the garden off, like. And it's exactly where she fell.' He pointed to the bench. 'Right there, it was. She was lying right there on the slabs.'

Not for the first time, Alice thought that Frank was a bit maladroit and actually a bit weird. Rather than responding to his comments, she said, 'Would you both like a drink? Perhaps you'd like to help yourselves. There's red or white wine, fruit juice or beer.' Alice took the opportunity to refresh her own glass and took a generous glug from it.

It was a few more minutes before Sarah, the last guest, arrived. Alice had almost given her up. Neil had spotted her first and was helping her to a drink. She was looking fresh and pretty in a full-skirted summery frock and sandals. Her large earrings bobbed gently as she talked to Neil. Alice wondered if she was late because she had spent extra time on her appearance. Alice went up to say hello and was favoured with a smile and Sarah's opinion that the bench was very nice.

Alice excused herself and poured another half glass of wine for herself. She noticed that no-one sat on the bench, but rather the attendees stole covert looks at it from time to time. The guests were clearly waiting for something to happen. It's time, thought Alice. She cast her eye over the group. Everyone had their glass charged and they were chatting together. It occurred to her that, apart from Carl, almost certainly it was one of these people who had taken Mum's ring, and then they had thought better of it and returned it, probably because they had found out it was worthless. No, she mustn't think of that now, she must focus on the task in hand or her courage would fail her. She took a deep breath and felt a surge of adrenaline come to her aid. That had always happened to her in her professional life: in the final seconds before addressing a group of people at a seminar or in a meeting, when it was too late to back out, the blessed internal drug would do its work by vanquishing the nerves and enable her to rise to the challenge of the task.

She walked to stand next to the bench, head held high, raised her voice and said, 'Hi everybody. First of all, thank you for coming out this evening to honour Lucy, my mother, by witnessing the dedication of this bench to her memory. I know that sounds a bit formal, but it means a lot to me that there is something to remember her by, instead of a grave. Since I came here a month ago you have all been so friendly and so kind. Mum had told me how much you were a little community here, and I gathered that she facilitated a good deal of the bonding of the group herself with her get-togethers. Oh yes, I used to hear all about them in our weekly Zoom calls.'

Alice saw slightly tentative smiles appear on most of the faces and she pressed on. 'You can imagine, it was a tremendous shock to me when Mum died so suddenly. I derived a great deal of comfort from being able to stay in Mum's flat for nearly a month. Although it was sad, I felt that staying where she had lived, and experiencing her home first hand, brought me closer to her. And it gave me a stable base for making all the arrangements that had to be done and for disposing of her possessions. So thank you, Carrie, for allowing that.

'I knew that there had been some vague talk about the garden needing something like a bench to set it off. And then when Neil suggested actually buying a bench as a memorial to Mum, the idea seemed perfect. Thank you, Neil.' He acknowledged her words with a quick wave. Now that she was at the top of her game, she was experienced enough to know that there was a danger of her running on for too long. So, she brought her speech to an end by saying, 'And it will be a comfort to me when I go home to know that there is something tangible to mark Mum's passing, and what better place to put it than in the garden of The Beeches, the place where she lived her last years. So, here's to Lucy.' She raised her glass to drink, and everyone joined her in the toast.

Alice sat down with a flourish on the bench. Charlie scampered up to sit beside her, while a spontaneous round of applause erupted from all the others. Alice felt euphoric. Her speech could have gone horribly wrong, and she could have become ambushed by emotion. But she wasn't. Neil sat down on the other side of her. 'Well done, babe,' he said. 'That was terrific. You totally nailed it.'

She turned her face to his and they kissed joyfully. This sparked off more cheering and clapping, led by Lesley and Jane. Alice turned to look at them all again, just in time to catch Sarah's aghast expression. She slammed her half-drunk glass of wine down on the table and left the gathering without a word.

'Alice,' said Charlie, tapping her on the leg. 'Jane said you're going away soon on a big aeroplane.'

'That's right,' said Alice. 'Have you ever been on an aeroplane?'

Charlie shook his head. 'Will you come back?' he said.

Alice knew you had to be honest with kids. 'I don't know for sure, Charlie. But I think I might.'

*

Already the new bench looks like it belongs here, thought Alice the next morning, as she looked out at it through the French doors. She heard from the kitchen the unmistakeable sound of the toaster popping up. Neil had heard it too because he came into the kitchen smoothing down his tie, which was part of what Alice now called his 'online uniform' – shirt, tie, shorts and bare feet. He came up behind her while she was buttering the crunchy toast and gave her a squeeze.

'I've got to be quick,' he said, reaching round her and grabbing a piece of toast. 'I've got a meeting in ten minutes.' He took a giant bite. 'I won't be more than two hours, though, and then we can go out for our hike.' His voice was muffled through his chewing.

'I'm looking forward to it,' said Alice, resolutely putting out of her mind how little time they had left.

'You're still on cloud nine, aren't you?' said Neil.

Alice brushed toast crumbs off his shirt front. 'I've got to admit, I'm still feeling pretty pleased with how things went.'

'And indeed you should be. You did fantastic. Everybody thought so.'

'Everybody except Sarah. She wasn't the least bit impressed when you kissed me.'

'Ah, like I said last night, who cares what she thinks. Babe, I must get started now. I'll see you later.'

Alice gathered up her things and let herself out quietly. She sauntered out onto the patio and sat down on the bench after reading the dedication plaque again. She was memorising everything about the scene while she still could. She took the ring out and frowned at it. Its five sparkly stones looked cheap and tawdry to her now. Why couldn't she just let the matter rest? She turned the camera app on her phone to its highest magnification and tried to focus on the ring, on its fake stones in their settings. If she left now, there would be enough time to go into town and be back when Neil was finishing his meeting. Yes, she would go to Branson and Son's one more time.

*

The little shop was familiar to her now. There were several jewellers' shops in the town, but she was glad she had chosen this one, even though the outcome hadn't been what she was expecting. This time she didn't have to wait, and Mr Branson greeted her straightaway.

'Good morning,' he said, his friendly smile indicating that he remembered her. He was looking smart in an old-fashioned way, with his waistcoat over his shirt and tie.

'Hello,' said Alice. 'Yes, it's me again. The lady with the fake family heirloom ring.' She tried to make light of her visit. 'The thing is, you see, I was just wondering…' She got the ring out of her bag and pulled herself together. 'The fact is, Mr Branson, I was wondering if an experienced jeweller like you would be able to tell if the ring had ever been tampered with? What I mean is, if the original stones have been removed and replaced with the fakes that we see here?'

She passed the ring over to Mr Branson and he gave it a cursory glance. 'Yes, it's possible to tell. You see, the stones are usually held in place by claws, like you see here. You can examine the claws with a microscope, and do other tests if needed, such as microhardness, to see if the claws have been retipped or if there is any sign of soldering.'

'I see. Would it be possible for you to do that now? I don't have much time, you see.'

Mr Branson passed the ring back to Alice and shook his head, rather smugly, she thought. 'No need. I already did that when you brought it in before. I can say definitely that this ring is in its original condition with the original stones.'

'Oh.' Alice wasn't sure if that was what she wanted to hear or not. At least now she knew the true, corrected story of the ring's past. But did the thief know it was a fake? And did it actually matter now?

Alice was just trying to get her head around this news when she heard the door of the shop open. 'Hello, Dad,' said Mr Branson. 'I wasn't expecting to see you today.'

'I had to pop out to get something for your mother, so I thought I'd look in.' Mr Branson senior was wearing a tweed overcoat, despite the warmth of the day. He went around to the other side of the counter, next to his son, and nodded cordially to Alice. Straightaway Alice could see the likeness between the two men: although Mr Branson senior had greyer hair and was more stooped that his son, they both had the same blue eyes and shape of the jaw.

'Ah, yes,' I remember that piece. May I?' Mr Branson senior took the ring from Alice and examined it closely. 'Very strange, as I recall.' He passed the ring back to Alice.

'What was strange, Dad?'

'Well, someone brought it in to be valued. Then before I could answer him properly, he snatched it back off me and practically ran out of the shop. It was most odd.'

*

Alice could hardly contain herself when she got back to Neil's flat. The mystery of who took Mum's ring solved at the eleventh hour! She could have guessed who it was. Of all The Beeches crew, it was only Frank who was shifty. Now the case could be closed and she could rest easy.

She burst into the flat and found Neil taking off his tie. 'I've just finished,' he said. 'We're free to set off when you're ready.' He caught sight of her expression. 'Whatever's the matter?'

Alice grabbed him by the arms. 'You'll never guess! I decided to go back to the jewellers shop one last time, to see if the ring had ever had the stones in it replaced. It turns out it hadn't, but that's not the most important thing.' She realised she was gabbling.

'OK,' said Neil. 'Take some deep breaths and try to tell me slowly. What's happened?'

Alice managed to calm herself down 'I was about to leave the shop when the old man, the one who must have been the original owner, came in and said he remembered seeing the ring before. A man had brought it in to be valued but then changed his mind and left abruptly. Don't you see, Neil? A man! That means it must have been Frank! I knew there was something fishy about him. And apparently his van was outside on the morning that Mum died. He told me he was there to do a job next door. I'm going to confront him and see what he has to say.'

'Alice, stop.' Neil's voice cut roughly across hers. 'It wasn't Frank who took Lucy's ring.'

'But…'

Neil removed her hands from his arms. 'It wasn't Frank. It was me.'

Chapter 14

On that fateful Saturday six weeks ago, Neil had woken early. His first thought, as he yawned and turned over, was to wonder whether he had any early meetings this morning? By the time he'd blinked a couple of times, he'd remembered that it was the weekend and of course he didn't have a work schedule. Yay! He reached his arms above his head, stretched luxuriously and thought about the day ahead. His mind clicked into gear, and he reviewed his agenda. First off, he'd arranged a game of tennis with his friend George at ten o'clock. Then there was Lucy's Garden party that she had invited him to, which was later in the afternoon. Quite a pleasant day in prospect.

Then he remembered that he'd told Lucy he would come to the party armed with prosecco, and that everybody was supposed to contribute something to eat. So he'd have to fit in a trip to the store later, after he and George had chilled out with a Coke and a chat in the park when they'd finished their match. In which case, with quite a few things to do, he'd better get moving. He rolled out of bed and scratched his naked belly, his morning erection subsiding as he moved to the bathroom.

George was already waiting for him when he turned up at the park, even though he wasn't late. The two friends clasped hands briefly and enquired after each other's health. Then without much preliminary talk, because the booking was only for an hour, they took up their positions at either end of the court and started knocking up. George had been on the same course as Neil when they were both in business school. The two men had stayed loosely in touch ever since, mainly because they lived in the same town, so it was a no-brainer that they should meet up again after Neil came back from New York. They used to play tennis sometimes back in the day, and George would almost inevitably win. Today, some twenty-five years on, nothing had changed, and Neil found himself on the receiving end of a thrashing, which had been the same story when he'd played with George a couple of weeks ago. Still, it was a good workout and a worthy match. Neil acknowledged that George was the better player and congratulated his friend on the result.

'But you kept me on my toes,' said George. 'It wasn't a walkover.' He poured some of his water bottle over his head and towelled his hair off. 'Park café OK?'

They sat down on the café terrace with two cans of fizzy drink each. After slaking his initial thirst, Neil duly asked after George's wife and two kids, whom he'd met a couple of times before he went to New York. George filled him in on his own news, before passing the conversational ball back and asking what was happening with Neil since they'd last met.

'Oh, everything's pretty good really. As I'd said, I've settled into the job, and I've got to say it becomes more and more apparent that I've really fallen on my feet with the place I'm renting. For instance, this afternoon Lucy, that's the woman in the flat next to mine, is throwing a mini party in the communal garden. All the residents are invited, I think, plus the gardener and the rep from the letting agency. This is the first time for me at one of these residents' get togethers, so I thought I'd take some bottles of prosecco. You know, so nobody can say the new guy is cheap.'

'And to get your feet under the table, eh? How old is she, this Lucy woman?'

'About seventy or so, I'd say. She's a young seventy though, and she's really made me welcome in the building.'

George raised his eyebrows. 'A party given by a septuagenarian, you say? You're really living on the wild side, aren't you, bro?'

'You've got the wrong idea. Lucy is just the enabler. This is a 'bond with your neighbours' kinda trip. Since I don't know many people, it's not a bad idea for me. And Lucy – she's nice. Sort of homey and welcoming. She's been good to me, anyway, when I was finding my way when I first got here.' Neil tried not to sound defensive.

'Rather you than me. I can't say I want to socialise much with the families on my road.'

'I guess it different if you're single and in a small community with a communal driveway, you can't help running into neighbours.' Neil took another glug of his first Coke and supressed a burp. 'Not that all the residents are living solo. There's two women living together in the front flat. They've got a kid.' It was predictable that that would get George's attention, so Neil filled him in on all the details, so far as he knew them. George also wanted to know what Sarah and even Carrie were like.

'So, what are you doing for fun nowadays, mate? Anything on the horizon?' said George.

'To be honest, I've been busy settling in since I came back. Getting my job on track and all that. It seems like a good company to work for.' Neil hoped that would deflect George's interest.

No such luck. 'Tell you what, let's go out next weekend and get shitfaced. I can be your wingman,' said George.

Neil told his friend exactly where he could stick that idea. He could get himself out there in his own way and in his own time.

George got the message and backed off. 'Seriously, are you here for good? What about that woman back in New York you told me about? Is that permanently over, or did you just need a break?'

Neil shook his head and feigned indifference. He fixed his gaze across the park where a small pond gleamed in the sunshine. A couple of children were zooming past on scooters. 'Diana? That's history now. She's got someone else. A big black dude. I saw them together on Facebook.'

'Sorry, man.' They both drank in silence for a few minutes while the summery ambience of the park floated around them.

'I've often wondered why you never settled down and got married.' Geoge was more tentative now. 'I mean, you don't seem to have any obvious obnoxious habits – not many, anyway – and you haven't exactly lived the life of a monk, have you?'

'Nope. I guess it's the old story that I've never met the right woman. It's been on the cards sometime, but there's always been something wrong.' Neil looked at his watch and stood up. 'Hey, is that the time? I should shoot.' He still had plenty of time, but the truth was that he wanted out from this conversation. 'Perhaps we can get a tennis rematch sometime soon if the weather holds? And I'm up for a night out with you. But no more of that wingman crap. I'm more than capable.'

*

Neil lay back on his bed with his arms behind his head. He could hear Charlie still scampering around the patio and playing some intricate game. He heard one of his mommies – he wasn't sure if it was Jane or Lesley – telling him it was time to come and have a bath and get ready for bed. Charlie resisted and was told firmly that he could have five more minutes and that was all. Lucy's party had been a winner. Neil wondered if her gatherings were always like that or if his plentiful supply of prosecco had given some extra social lubrication to the event.

Neil ran his mind over the little company. He had met everyone before, but it had been OK to get to know them a little more. He'd talked with all of them, and even Frank had relaxed and become garrulous after two or three glasses of wine. Lucy had seemed a little tired by the end, but then, she was almost an old lady, and it must have been a lot of work for her. He had cheerfully helped with the clearing up, like they all had, while Lucy sat down on her sofa and took it easy.

So now what? He had no dinner plans for this evening. For the first time since coming to The Beeches he felt a little lonely, in fact. There should be no reason for that, he told himself. In his mind he recited once more the inventory of his fulfilling life. His job was going well, he kept fit, played sport, and had several friends. He could even drive for a few hours and see his brother, if he was desperate. And look at today, for instance. He'd played a game of tennis, hung out with a buddy and then gone to a garden party where he was fairly sure the two non-lesbian women were giving him the eye. Perhaps he could just phone for take-out and watch a movie on Netflix.

And yet. And yet George's comments, well-meaning though they were, had struck a chord. When he came back to England, he wondered – hoped, maybe – if, after his six-month lease was over, he might be heading back to the States and he and Diana might give their relationship another go. That wasn't looking to be on the cards now, since he was slammed with that Facebook post yesterday that showed her living it large on a Caribbean cruise with lover boy. Meanwhile Neil could convince himself he was doing OK: he was definitely getting settled here, even though in some ways he missed the pulse of New York. If he wanted bright lights and big city buzz, London wasn't too far away. So he should do himself a favour and admit that Diana had moved on, and so should he. Easy enough to say.

Another tangible disappointment in his new life here was that his efforts to set up his own on-line business looked like being a non-starter. But then, if he was honest, his main motivation had been to make some extra money to impress Diana. He sighed and sat up on the edge of his bed. He could stop beating that particular dead horse, then, and let it go. Quite a relief, really. And yeah, it wouldn't be a bad idea to get into the dating scene again. His mind went back to Carrie, long-legged and perky, and Sarah, quite pretty when you got her to relax. He was sure he could pull either of those if he put his mind to it. But close to home like that? Bad idea. George's question about why he had never settled down, he chose to ignore. It had just never happened for him, that's all.

The heady effects of the prosecco were beginning to wear off. He checked his watch. Eight-thirty. In these light summer evenings, it could be hard to guess the time. What to do now? He could get an Uber into town and top up his alcohol level while he got some supper somewhere, perhaps a curry. Or plan B was the take-out and movie option. Perhaps he should procrastinate some more before making a decision. He lay back down on the bed, picked up his phone and began to check his messages and browse social media.

And there she was again. Why hadn't he just unfriended her from his Facebook? He knew why, of course. He wanted to see what she was up to. This time she was showing off a classy diamond necklace that lover boy had just bought her, apparently. She was smiling her delight, and he had his arms around her from behind while one hand had picked up the sparklies to show them off. Is that what it takes with you, Diana? How much does it take to buy you? More than I've got, apparently.

Neil flung himself off the bed and yanked off his tee shirt and shorts. He sprayed his armpits liberally with deodorant. That would have to do. A fresh shirt, trousers and shoes. He checked his pocket for his wallet, thrust his phone in his other pocket, and strode out of his flat, slamming the door behind him.

*

The throb in his head was excruciating. Neil's eyelids fluttered open. The pale light didn't help so he closed them again. He became aware that he was face down on top of his bed and fully dressed, including his shoes. He tried to move his head but soon thought better of it; he tried to swallow, but his mouth and throat were totally dry, so he thought better of that too. And what was all that noise coming from outside, early on a Sunday morning? He could hear various voices; he could hear men's voices. Who were they? He risked opening his eyes again and gathered it was still early in the morning. Oh no, and now he wanted a pee so he would have to move.

With considerable groaning Neil dragged himself to the toilet. After peeing he staggered to the kitchen and drew himself a pint of water, slopping it everywhere in the process. He managed to swallow it straight down, apart from what he spilled down his chin. Once back on his bed he pulled his shoes and trousers off. Anything else was just too much effort. Neil slept.

*

When he woke up sunlight was streaming in through the bedroom window, because the curtains had been left open all night. For several minutes he blinked at the sunny streaks on the ceiling and let the disorientation inhabit him. His head still ached abominably, and his mouth was still dry, but neither was as bad as it had been earlier. What had all that noise been? Did he dream it? He wasn't sure. It probably wasn't important. Anyway, he couldn't be bothered to care right now.

He looked at his watch. It was coming up to midday. He probably wouldn't sleep any more now. It would be a good idea to glug a bottle of rehydration drink. He'd learned that trick in the past: the same drink that he used after a long run or strenuous sport served equally well to fix a hangover. This wasn't the first hangover he'd had, but it was certainly one of the worst, if not the worst.

The electrolyte drink and a long cool shower to wash off last night's staleness did a lot to accelerate the recovery process. Neil sat at his kitchen table and contemplated a couple of pieces of toast to go with his orange juice. Only after he'd gingerly munched his way through the first piece did he allow himself to ruminate on the events of the previous evening and night. It was rare for him to have memory blank from too much alcohol, but this time his recall of the later parts of his night out was certainly hazy.

He had no problem remembering the first part of the evening. He had sat in a pub, eaten steak and ale pie with chips, half watched a game of pool that was going on, and then half watched the football match that was onscreen with the sound turned down. He accompanied all that with a couple of pints of beer – or was it three? – and sat there until he was chucked out with the others at closing time. He had faced the fact, painfully, that Diana had moved on and that he was unlikely to get her back, especially since he couldn't afford expensive presents to woo her with.

Conveniently, it was only a short way down the street to the nightclub entrance, a low-key door that you'd walk straight past in the daytime. A couple of guys that he had talked to in the pub had assured him that it was a place that did the job and that he wouldn't go home alone. Neil was glad he hadn't left it any later, because a queue was starting to form on the street. The two doormen were checking everyone out, particularly the men. Neil knew he was pretty safe because he was dressed smart casual, not too drunk and in the right age group – that is, not young. Once inside he let his eyes adjust to the dark and went up to the bar. The DJ was hunched over his control deck and the music he was playing was nothing Neil recognised.

During the next couple of hours, the place filled up, and the dance floor started to see some action. Neil was one of several men who hovered on the periphery and eyed up the women with their short skirts and long flowing hair. He noted that, whereas the majority of the clubbers were probably in their thirties, there were a few saddoes like him who were in their late forties or even more. After a while Neil's attention homed in on a group of women who were hanging out by the bar when they weren't dancing. He tried making eye contact with one, a pert blonde who looked to be in her thirties. His smile was met with a slightly questioning look before she turned away to talk to her friends. God, how out of practice he was with all this. Still, he knew he had good looks and a toned physique on his side. After a while of playing the eye contact and smiling game he sauntered up to blondie and asked if he could buy her a drink. She asked for some expensive cocktail.

Then what happened? He remembered dancing and didn't care what he looked like. A sure sign that he was drunk. He knew he'd asked blondie her name, but he was ashamed to say that he couldn't remember what it was. Maddie? Maxine? It might not even have begun with M. To be honest, he couldn't hear every word that she said because of the loud music, and a lot of their conversation involved him nodding eagerly. Towards the end of the night there had been some snogging and a bit of groping, with considerable enthusiasm on both sides. At that point the evening had been going well.

The night was starting to wind down when Neil made the necessary visit to the men's room to buy a packet of condoms from the machine there. He was now most definitely drunk. He was aware he had to concentrate to walk in a straight line. He didn't think he'd have any trouble performing, though, judging from the hard-on he'd had while he had his tongue down her throat. And it had been a long time.

Neil was smiling in anticipation as he stashed his purchase in his pocket and made his somewhat unsteady way back into the club. But he couldn't find blondie. He hung around uncertainly outside the women's toilets while the DJ dismantled his equipment and people made their way out into the night, in couples, groups, or dejectedly alone. There she was, in the taxi queue with her pals. His last view of her was her backside when she climbed into the cab and he was left standing on the pavement like an idiot. What had he done wrong?

After that the night went downhill. His memory of events was hazy and riddled with black gaps. Neil sat at his kitchen table the next morning with his crumb-littered toast plate and his orange juice glass empty and forced himself to try to reconstruct events. He knew he had staggered to an all-night convenience store and bought a small bottle of whiskey – not a smart move after all the booze he'd already had. He couldn't really remember where he was when the streetwalker had approached him or what conversation they had had, if any. He didn't try too hard to remember what happened next. There were recollections of a dingy room, a fetid smell and the bored, featureless hooker. It had been the one and only time in Neil's life that he had visited a prostitute, and he was now thoroughly ashamed of himself.

Presumably, a taxi brought him home and he managed to get into his flat unaided, although he didn't know how. Fleeting half images scudded across the screen of his mind, and he wasn't sure if they were dream fragments or real occurrences. The capering figures of women on the dance floor, streetlights rushing past the taxi, the coolness of the garden with the first screech of the dawn chorus, the dim shapes of bushes and other shapes in the lifting grey dawn. These impressions all jumbled in his mind. Why was he in the garden at dawn? Just wandering, presumably. There was something else, but he couldn't grasp it. The more he tried, the further it receded.

Oh God. Neil buried his face in his hands and tried to block it all out. Then a disturbing thought occurred to him, and he lurched up to grab his trousers from where they lay on the bedroom floor. He fumbled in the pocket and pulled out the packet of condoms. There was one missing. Thank goodness! At least he hadn't had unprotected sex with a whore. Wait a minute, what else was this in his pocket? He pulled out a five-stoned ring which looked like diamonds. He stared at it, dumbfounded and puzzled. Something tugged at his memory, but he didn't quite know what. He sat back down at the table and frowned at the ring in front of him. He had seen it somewhere before. He thought hard. Yes… yes of course. Lucy had a ring like that. She had shown it to him once. In a flash of inspiration, he pulled out his phone and found the photo he had taken at her gathering yesterday. It was a close-up of Lucy holding a glass of prosecco. The ring was clearly visible on her hand. I'll take it back to her, Neil thought. Although I don't know what I'm going to say about why I've got it. I just don't remember.

*

Lucy wasn't there when Neil knocked on her door later that day. He went round again to return the ring the next morning, Monday, by which time he was feeling his normal self again. He was surprised to see that her door was open, and Carrie was just coming out.

'Oh…' he said. 'I called to see Lucy. Is she there?'

Carrie's expression was grave. 'So you haven't heard?' she said.

Chapter 15

Alice had to sit down. She slumped in the chair and put her head into her hands. No, no, this couldn't be true, what Neil had just told her. She was aware of him standing awkwardly beside her. She felt his hand placed tentatively on her shoulder and she shook it off.

'Let me see if I've got this right,' said Alice through her hands. 'You're telling me that you think you took Mum's ring when you were drunk, but you can't actually remember doing it. Is that what you're saying?'

She dropped her hands and looked directly at Neil. He was the picture of distress.

'That's exactly what I'm saying, Alice. I know how improbable it sounds, but that's how it must have been. When I found the ring in my pocket the next morning, I just couldn't get my head round it. There was something vaguely in the back of my mind about being in the garden when it was just getting light… but that's all I could remember. The rest is just a blank. And the next day I had a hangover like you wouldn't believe.'

'Oh, poor you.' Alice didn't bother to keep the sarcasm out of her voice. 'So you expect me to believe that you took the ring right off her finger where she lay there dead?'

Neil groaned and flopped down on the chair next to Alice. 'I don't know for certain, as knowing goes. He spread his hands helplessly. 'I know it sounds far-fetched, but I think that's the only thing that could have happened.'

'And run it by me one more time, why you got so drunk.'

'Well, I'd been drinking in the afternoon at your mom's party. Then I decided to go out and get some supper. I'll level with you – a friend had been goading me that morning about why I hadn't gotten myself a girlfriend yet. I guess I'd been thinking – hoping, maybe – that after we'd had a break, Diana and I might give it another go.' Neil passed his hand over his haggard face. 'Anyway, before I went out, I checked my social media and there she was, this time wearing some even more expensive jewellery that was a present from her new lover. Well, it hit me in the face that I couldn't compete in those stakes, and also that my hopes for an online business venture were going belly up, and basically, I was nothing but a loser. And Diana was a gold-digger. That was the frame of mind I was in when I went out.'

Alice waited, her face averted from him. When he didn't speak, she said, 'So you went out determined to get laid, and it all went wrong. That's what you told me, isn't it?'

Neil squirmed. 'Yes, that's about it. You don't need to know all the sordid details, but the bottom line was I got more drunk than I'd ever been in my life. I was lucky I managed to get home without being mugged or something.'

Alice sensed that he wasn't telling her everything about his evening, but she decided she didn't want to know.

'Then you posted the ring back through my door, anonymously, on the day after Mom's funeral. What was all that about?'

'I know. Pathetic, isn't it? You see, I didn't know what to do about the situation. I'd met you by then and I liked you. Do you remember when I came round to meet you and pay my respects, and I started to cry? That wasn't just about grief for Lucy. It was about the fact that I'd got her ring and didn't know what to do.'

'Why didn't you just tell me then?'

'Oh, come on Alice, how could I? How was I going to explain something that sounded so incredible, even to me? I thought if I just kept quiet about it, you'd never realise. But then I saw more of you at Lucy's funeral. You made quite an impression on me, Alice. Oh, I don't mean that I fancied you. Not then, anyway. That would have been quite improper. I mean, you were so dignified, so... so... I don't know, poised and composed, perhaps. Lucy used to talk about you, you know. She was obviously very proud of you. Sure, she showed me photos as well, but it was more about the sort of woman that she described. She told me how you'd made a career and a life for yourself out in Australia and picked yourself up after your marriage broke down. You seemed like a very together person. I never dreamed that I'd meet you.'

Alice felt somewhat mollified by what Neil said about how Mum had portrayed her. Was he speaking sincerely, or was he saying exactly the right things to soften her towards him? She dragged her mind back from the poignant image of Mum sitting in her flat with Neil to the topic in hand. 'But I still don't understand why you put the ring back through my door. Why, Neil?'

Neil groaned. 'Oh Alice, I can see in hindsight that it was the wrong thing to do. I guess I just panicked. Once I saw you at Lucy's funeral, I knew it was only right that you should have the ring back. It was important and, after all, it was your property. Somehow, I persuaded myself that you'd just accept that the ring had been mislaid and be glad that it had been found. I didn't suspect for one minute that you'd try to find out who had taken it.'

Alice was scathing. 'You didn't? That was stupid of you not to realise that.'

Neil hung his head. 'Yes, it was. Totally stupid. I didn't think it through.'

They both fell silent. Alice felt drained. That Neil, her lover, would be the one who had taken her mother's ring was the last thing she would have suspected, and she was having a hard time getting her head around what he had told her. Suddenly the room, laden with emotion as it had become, was unbearably claustrophobic. She had to get out. 'I'm going outside,' she said. 'On my own.'

*

The bench was sited in the sun and so, when Alice sat down on it, heat spread to her back and legs and to her arm where it lay along the armrest. If she listened carefully, she could hear gentle gurgling noises coming from the little river as it made its way downstream. The sounds mingled with the odd chirrup of birdsong overhead.

True, there was a background of intermittent traffic noise, but as the road was at the other side of The Beeches, the noise was muted and ignorable. The day was warm but not hot, and the sunshine was pleasant rather than oppressive. The varied bushes and trees fluttered their leaves in the breeze and tongues of weeds were insinuating themselves insistently through the gaps between the flagstones on the patio. Alice started to feel soothed by these sensations of nature. In two days' time, she said to herself, you'll be travelling to the airport. Before too long all this will be just a memory. All of it.

'Hello,' said Charlie, who seemed to materialise in front of her. 'I've come out to play.'

'Oh… hello, Charlie. I didn't hear you. I was thinking.'

Charlie was wearing his normal summer attire of shorts and tee shirt. Today his tee shirt featured three dinosaurs. 'What were you thinking about?' he said.

'I was thinking that soon I'll be getting on a big aeroplane and going home,' said Alice, truthfully.

'I like aeroplanes,' said Charlie, and he stretched his arms out and zoomed about the garden making creditable aeroplane noises.

Jane came around the corner and spotted Alice. 'Hi, Alice. Is he annoying you?'

'Hi, Jane. No, he's fine. He's being an aeroplane.'

'Of course,' said Jane. 'I should have guessed.' She plonked herself down on the bench beside Alice, kicked off her flip-flops and wiggled her toes. 'Anyway, how are you?'

Alice opened her mouth to reply conventionally that she was fine but found that she couldn't quite tell the lie. Jane would see through her, after all. She was good at that. 'I'm feeling a bit devastated at the moment, actually.'

'Oh? I'm sorry to hear that. What's happened?'

Alice hesitated. She wanted to open up to Jane, but she didn't know what to say. She tried to weigh up the options, but it all seemed so confused in her head. If she told the full story, it would seem pretty incredible. And then Jane would know that she and Lesley, and everyone in fact, had been under suspicion of taking the ring. Also, Neil had to go on living here after she herself had gone home.

Although, she wasn't too sure she cared about that.

Jane turned her gaze away to give Alice time to compose herself. She said, 'What a wonderfully peaceful little space this is. That is, until we had an aeroplane flying past. But it looks like it's come in to land.' Charlie was now sitting on the patio and crooning to himself. 'And this bench – well, it fits perfectly here. A totally fitting memorial to dear Lucy.' She smiled kindly at Alice. 'So, what's up?'

'I don't really want to go into all the details, but it's something with Neil.'

'I had a feeling it might be.'

'You see…' Alice struggled with what to say, without saying too much. 'You see, he kept something from me, something he should have told me. It's come as a bit of a shock.'

'Ah. And is it important, this something?'

Was it important, thought Alice, now that it's out in the open? 'It's fairly important,' she said. 'Let's say he made a mistake.'

'A mistake. Yes, people do that. They make mistakes. Can you forgive him?'

Alice shrugged her shoulders slowly. 'I honestly don't know.' She glanced up to meet Jane's eyes but realised that Jane was now looking beyond her towards Neil's flat. She turned to see what Jane was looking at, and she saw Neil standing inside his French window, looking about as mournful as a person could. He waved tentatively.

Jane stood up and called to Charlie. 'We've got to go now,' she said. 'Alice, I sincerely hope that you and Neil manage to patch this up before you go home. It would be such a shame to part on a bad note.' She leaned down and kissed Alice on the cheek.

*

Neil didn't attempt to touch Alice or to speak to her when she came back into the flat. They stood looking at each other in bewilderment. Eventually Neil said, 'I saw you talking to Jane.' When Alice continued to remain silent, he said, 'Oh Alice, tell me what I can do. How can I make it up to you? Just tell me. I am so, so sorry.'

'Yes, I think you are,' said Alice, bemused at her own calmness.

'I think it would be best if I went away. We need some time apart. I'll stay in a hotel, but I'll be back for my luggage.'

'No, no! please don't go! Neil shook his head in anguish. He tried to take her hands, but she put them behind her back. 'You see, Alice, I… I love you. I've fallen in love with you. I can't bear it if we part like this.'

Just yesterday Alice would have been over the moon to hear those words from Neil. Now she felt dismayed and confused. 'I will come back tomorrow, I promise,' she said. 'But I need some time on my own to process things right now.'

Neil tried to put his arms around her, but she stepped back and gently pushed his arms away. He licked his lips. 'I'll come to you. There's only a couple of months left on my lease here. I'll quit my job, and I'll come to Australia. I mean it, Alice.'

'Don't say any more now. You're only making me more confused. Let me think.' Alice put her hands up to her head, as if she could slow down the impressions she was being bombarded with. She went into the bathroom and gathered her toothbrush and basic toiletries. Then she went to the bedroom and pulled out her backpack, which was to be her hand luggage on the plane. She stuffed a change of clothes, along with her phone charger and other essentials, inside it. Neil watched her from the door, but he didn't attempt to stop her. Perhaps he too realised that the best course of action now was to let the emotionally charged situation cool down.

'You are coming back tomorrow, aren't you?' said Neil.

'Yes, said Alice. 'I've got to, haven't I, my luggage is here.' She hesitated, then added, 'We can talk some more then.'

That seemed to placate Neil. 'OK. Can I give you a lift to a hotel?'

'No, thank you,' said Alice. Before anything further could pass between them, she shouldered her backpack and was gone.

Chapter 16

Whereas Alice would have been willing to cook a turkey dinner on Christmas day for her mother, Mum always claimed she didn't want all that fuss. What she really liked was to go to a beach with a picnic or a barbie on Christmas day. It was such a treat, she used to say, to have all that sunshine and warmth in what was for her the middle of winter. So Alice, Lucy, Zoe and Joe would set off early to get a parking space and head for one of Sydney's beach spots. Even though Alice didn't select one of the most popular beaches, it would still be pretty packed. Alice had to admit, it wouldn't have been her choice of how to spend Christmas day, but her mum just loved it. Typically, the kids would wander off to meet up with their friends, and Alice and Mum would be left sitting on the rug talking, talking, talking. They never seemed to run out of things to say. There was no indication, no hint, last Christmas that it would indeed be the last Christmas that Alice would spend with her mother. Whatever am I going to do this year, thought Alice. I haven't even thought of that. Zoe and Joe probably won't want to spend very much time with me, especially since their Granny is not going to be there.

Alice was laid on her back on the bed in a hotel room, hands linked behind her head and staring at the ceiling where the smoke alarm blinked. The bed was enormous, because of course it was designed for two people. The bedding was snowy white, smooth and pristine. The furniture was the usual anodyne collection of TV, desk, office chair and wardrobe space. Being cocooned in that room gave no indication of whereabouts you were, apart from some clues in the information leaflet on the desk about the safe, air conditioning, room service menu and suchlike. Sounds of the outside world were excluded by the double glazing. Alice felt keenly in this space that she was suspended between the world she was trying to shake off and the familiar life which awaited her.

Oh Mum, I haven't thought about you much lately. But you know I haven't forgotten you. Alice silently addressed her mother, as if she was sitting in the room with her, nodding wisely. Alice acknowledged that her time with Neil had helped to soothe and regularise her grief. The worst, the sharpest of it was probably past now. No doubt when she got home there would be a hole where her Saturday morning chat with Mum had been. But that was not the only hole that there would be in her life.

Mum, Mum, what am I going to do about Neil? What would *you* do? We were going to pack so much into these last couple of days and now here I am, laid in a hotel room alone. She felt the tears start to slide down her cheeks towards her ears, so she turned over onto her side and curled up. Then she sobbed unrestrainedly into the accommodating white pillow until the outpouring subsided.

'One thing's for sure, Alice love, you don't want to just leave it. That way it's always going to bother you. Much better to get some sort of resolution.' Alice could hear what her mum would say, almost as if she was there and they were having a conversation.

'Yes, but what resolution? I was so shocked that he was the one who took your ring. Never in a million years would I have suspected that.' Alice spoke the words inside her head.

'Probably not. I always thought that he was a rather nice man. Decent, you know, but a bit lost. He didn't say much about it, but I think that last relationship of his broke him up. Until you came along, that is. And he liked my Welsh Cakes! Do you know what the best thing is you could do now, Alice?'

'No, but I'm sure you're going to tell me.'

'Forgive him. He did a wrong thing, but that doesn't mean he's a bad person. And he's truly sorry, isn't he? If you don't forgive him, you'll just keep the badness inside yourself. That's corrosive.'

Alice dried her tears and turned over on her back again. Speaking her thoughts internally in her mother's voice was having a comforting effect. 'I said I was going back tomorrow. Hopefully we might be able to patch it up then.'

'Yes, dear. If you want to wait that long. I don't know, all this fuss and palaver about a silly ring.'

A silly ring? thought Alice. Yes, if you wanted to put it like that. 'But he lied to me, Mum.'

'I don't think he actually lied to you – he just avoided telling you.'

'It amounts to the same thing.' But does it, really, thought Alice. She was starting to regret having booked into a hotel. Yet it was true that she had wanted a bit of time on her own to get her feelings straight. Although now it seemed such a long time on her own until tomorrow. She got her phone out to see if there had been a message or a call from Neil and she had missed it. Nothing.

Her mother chimed in again. 'Tell me, dear, I realise you haven't known Neil for very long, but do you think you love him?'

'Mind your own business, Mum,' was Alice's reply.

*

Had Alice but known it, the park café that she sat in later to eat an ice cream was the same one that Neil had been in with his friend George some weeks before. From her table she could see the pond with ducks and a couple of swans drifting serenely past on it. A couple of kids were chucking pieces of bread, rather inaccurately, towards the birds. They were obviously brother and sister because they were squabbling and pushing each other. Just like Zoe and Joe used to do, thought Alice. I'll be seeing them soon. The weekend after I'm back, if they're free. Alice's gloom lifted just a bit, then descended again when she thought of Neil and how she felt. How did she feel? Confused, mainly. She hadn't been so mind-blowingly attracted to a man since those heady days when she had met her husband and he had swept her off her feet. But then Neil had gone and ruined it. But it was a mistake, said another voice in her head. And he's sorry.

Alice licked her ice cream cone mindlessly. Chocolate was her favourite flavour, but today she didn't care how good it was. She checked her watch: nearly five o'clock. She left the café with its neat little tables, each with their own small vase of wildflowers. That was the sort of touch she would normally have noticed and which would have delighted her. As it was, she left the park and hardly took in anything around her, not even the birds pecking for crumbs on the winding paths.

Alice decided she might as well go back to her hotel, although she didn't know what she was going to do when she got there. She had only been back in her hotel room for five minutes when the phone rang, making her jump. Neil's name flashed up on the screen. Oh, thank God! He's rung! 'Hello,' she said, breathless with relief.

'Alice?' he said. 'I'm downstairs in the foyer. The guy on the desk won't let me through.'

'I'll come down and meet you now.' Alice just about remembered to grab her key before she flew down the stairs because she couldn't bear to wait for the lift. There he was, looking tousled and anguished. There was no hesitation from either of them, and she poured herself into his arms. She could feel his heart thumping strongly. Eventually they were able to disentangle themselves and Alice said, 'How did you know where to find me?'

Neil shrugged. 'I figured you'd probably head for the nearest decent hotel, so I took a shot on this one. I thought if I phoned, you might not answer or refuse to tell me where you were.' He stroked her cheek, and they ended up in an embrace again.

The desk clerk coughed to get their attention. 'I'd say "get a room" but it seems like you've already got one,' he said with a cheeky grin. 'I just need to add you on as a guest if you'll be staying the night, sir. And amend the charge, of course.'

'Will I be staying the night, do you think?' Neil said to Alice, with a straight face.

'You'd better,' replied Alice.

*

After they had attended to the formalities with the desk clerk, they closeted themselves in a corner of the hotel's bar and drank cold lagers. Alice felt too informally dressed to go out anywhere else.

Plus, she didn't want to go wandering the streets with Neil. For one thing her legs were unusually weak, and at the moment she wanted just to look at him. So they both readily agreed to stay in the hotel. This three-star hotel was part of a well-known chain, a household name for good value and comfort, but no frills. The bar, which was decorated in a plain style, was quiet as yet because it was early. Three or four lone business men and women were hunched over their phones or laptops, and an elderly couple sat side by side hardly speaking to each other.

Alice thirstily took a large mouthful of her lager. She wasn't usually a beer drinker, but when Neil asked her at the bar what she wanted, she had said she'd have what he was having. It was easier than thinking. But actually, it turned out to be just what she needed in that moment.

'I thought you might turn me away,' said Neil.

'Earlier today I would have done,' said Alice. 'I've had time to cool down now and be on my own to think.' She paused, then decided to go on. 'Actually, there's something I'm not clear on and I need to know. I want you to tell me the truth, Neil.' She looked him firmly in the eye.

'I promise I'll be upfront with you, Alice. That deception has caused nothing but trouble for both of us.'

'OK, here goes.' Alice took a deep breath. 'When you put the ring back through my door, had you already found out that it was not real diamonds, and was that the reason why you returned it? Because it was worthless?'

Neil's reply was instant. 'Absolutely not! You already heard from the guy in that little jewellery shop that I took it to him intending to get rid of it, but then I lost my nerve and ran out. That's how you found out that it was me who took the ring, if you remember. Honestly Alice, I swear. I was stunned when you told me it was a fake all along. You do believe me, don't you?'

Alice looked at him. His expression was earnest, anguished. She made her decision. 'Yes, I believe you.'

Neil gave a long sigh and took her hand. 'Thank you. Thank you, Alice. That means a lot.'

'But if you had sold the ring, what were you going to do with the money?'

'I didn't really know. I was confused. You can tell that by the fact that I bottled it and ran out of the shop.'

Alice considered the authenticity of this. Then she abruptly downed the rest of her beer, put her glass down firmly and said, 'I'm sick of this damned ring and this whole topic. Let's go upstairs and shower before we get something to eat.'

*

Alice, her wet hair very lightly towelled, lay back on the bed and thought how much nicer it was to have two people on the large expanse of bedding than just one. One person could get lost in the hugeness of such a bed. They lay secluded in their own thoughts, breathing quietly, their fingertips touching. The room was tidy and gleaming, because Neil didn't have any luggage at all and Alice had only a small backpack containing her overnight things. They had decided to stay the night in the hotel room because, after all, Alice had paid for it. The unfamiliar environment seemed to suit this next chapter in their relationship. The very short chapter which would end Friday morning.

'This time the day after tomorrow, I won't be here,' said Alice. 'It doesn't seem possible.'

'I know,' said Neil. 'I can't, or don't want, to believe it either. But you must be looking forward to seeing Zoe and Joe.'

'Yes, sort of,' said Alice. 'Yes, of course,' she amended. 'But they have their own lives now, and I don't figure much in them. 'I wish I could just see them for a time and then… and then come back to you.' There, I've said it now, thought Alice. While she was on a roll and before she lost her courage, she continued, 'And what you said this morning, did you mean it?'

'We both said a lot of things this morning, and yesterday. You'll have to be more specific.' Neil's twinkling eyes suggested that he was teasing her.

'You know what I mean. When you told me that you loved me.'

155

'The L-word? Did I really say that?' He was definitely teasing her now.

'You know you did! The thing is…'

'Yes?'

'The thing is, I love you too. I know it's crazy, but I do. I've fallen in love with you.' Suddenly there was no more teasing.

'What are we going to do?' said Alice.

'Let's not talk about it now,' Neil said. I've bought something for you this afternoon, Alice. I was going to give it to you tomorrow but on second thoughts I'd like you to have it now and you can wear it at dinner.' Neil reached into his pocket and pulled out a small parcel. Alice sat up on the bed expectantly. A present! What woman didn't like to receive a present? 'Please understand that this doesn't signify a proposal of marriage,' Neil said. 'It's just… well, you'll understand.'

Within the parcel was a small box. Within the box was a ring, with a diamond and two sapphires.

Chapter 17

They had just got back to Neil's flat the following morning when a message arrived on Alice's phone:

Hi Alice, I know you're going home tomorrow, so just wondered if you'd like to pop round to ours for a cup of coffee, so that we can say goodbye and wish you well? Jane x

'Actually, I'd quite like to go. Just for a short time. Could we?' said Alice.

'Oh,' said Neil, his face registering his disappointment. 'This is our last full day.'

'I know. But Jane has been kind to me, so I'd like say goodbye. When you and I fell out yesterday and I was in the garden, she helped me and was kind. And she helped me when I first arrived here after Mum had just died.'

Neil looked alarmed. 'You didn't tell her what the argument was about, did you?'

'No, of course not. She just knew we'd had a… misunderstanding.'

'OK, let's do it. But not too long so we can go out somewhere for the rest of the day.'

Jane's face broke into a smile when she saw that it was Alice on her doorstep. Her smile became even broader when she saw that Neil was there too. As they stepped in Alice was able to decode Jane's subtle question conveyed by the slight raising of her eyebrows. Alice responded with a small nod and a joyous smile. This interplay between the two women was made easier because Neil had been spotted by Charlie who had promptly dragged him off to see his little train set.

'I see that Charlie's train set has got a fan,' called Jane from the kitchen as she drew water into the kettle.

'Are you kidding?' said Neil from where he was sitting cross-legged on the carpet. He didn't take his eyes from the locomotive as it chugged its way round the track. 'I love train sets! My brother and I used to share one when we were boys.'

'Make sure you let Neil have a turn,' said Jane to Charlie. 'You know what we said about sharing.' The two women settled down at the table with their drinks.

'Can I show you the surprise present that Neil has bought me?' Alice held out her right hand and wriggled her fingers to show off the twinkling single diamond flanked by two sapphires. 'It's a modern design and setting rather than a traditional one.'

Jane gasped with admiration and took a photo of Alice wearing it so that she could show it to Lesley, who was at work. With her usual tact, Jane didn't bombard Alice with questions about the gift and its significance. What a nice person she is, thought Alice.

Charlie and Neil joined them at the table and Charlie grabbed a biscuit. 'We saw the little town yesterday,' he said.

'What little town, mate?' said Neil.

Charlie couldn't quite remember what it was called, but after some prompting from Jane, he told them that it was called a model village. 'With little houses and little people and a little railway and everything,' he said, clearly enthusiastic.

'It was a super day out,' said Jane, 'And less than an hour away. The whole place was a really good representation of how things were in my childhood. I think I enjoyed it as much as Charlie did.'

'We should go there for our trip today,' said Neil suddenly, looking at Alice. Go back to your childhood and my childhood. And it's got a model railway! Let's go!'

*

'What a great idea this was,' said Alice as they sat on the grass in the model village. It struck her as sedate and charming. Within easy view for them was a miniature lake with a bridge and cars, streets and shops, a farm, and of course the railway track with a train that stopped at the station. Alice was filled with nostalgia at the tiny reproduction of places that seemed to be straight out of her childhood. There were plenty of people gazing at the well-planned scenes and, to be fair, there were more adults than children.

'Did your parents bring you to a place like this when you were a kid? I know mine did,' said Neil.

Alice frowned, trying to remember. 'Yes, I'm sure they did. I don't think there's many in Wales, so it must have been on holiday.'

'Mm. It's pretty much a British thing, right? So, it's neat that we both have the same sort of memories. I don't mean model villages, I mean of the way things were in our young days in general. We haven't had much chance to talk about our upbringings, our schools and our homes. Yet.' The final word hung in the air. When Alice didn't reply, Neil added, 'I meant it when I said I can come to Australia. There's a couple more months left on my rental agreement, and I would only need to give a month's notice in my job. Say yes, Alice, say yes.'

'But…' Alice tried to take in the enormity of the prospect that was opening up before her. Neil in Sydney with her? Yes, she loved him, so it was wonderful to think that they would be together. But being sensible, would it work? What if it didn't? After all, she had thought that she and Dan were for ever, but it didn't turn out that way.

As if guessing her thoughts, Neil said 'Look, I'm not suggesting anything permanent. At least, not to start with. What if I just come for a few months? I can sort out all the visa stuff, and then I should be able to get a temporary job. I can turn my hand to lots of things, you know, not just accountancy. And I'd find somewhere to stay on my own, if that's what you'd prefer. What do you say, Alice?'

'My house is big enough. You could stay with me. But Neil, what if it doesn't work?'

'If it doesn't work after a few months then at least we'll know we tried.'

Alice allowed herself to surrender. 'OK, let's do it.'

Several heads in the model village had turned to see a man

whooping and capering around on the grass and pulling a woman to her feet to dance with him.

*

They had thought that they would have gone out for a slap-up meal because it was Alice's final evening, but when it came to it, neither of them could be bothered to go out. Instead, they lounged around in Neil's flat, drank wine, ate pizza and talked about their newly forming plans.

'I never was completely settled here in England,' said Neil. 'That's why I only took a flat for six months. To be honest, I secretly hoped I might be heading back to New York.'

'You mean, you thought you might get back together with your old girlfriend? Diana, isn't it?'

'I thought it was possible. But then I met you, and she faded like a shadow.'

Alice basked in the compliment and felt she could afford to be magnanimous. 'I hope you were happy with her for a while.'

'Yeah, I guess. It seems insubstantial, like a dream now. And all my other girlfriends.'

'*All* your other girlfriends? There's been a lot, then?'

'Well, several. Let's be honest, we've both been round the track a few times. Which isn't a bad thing.' Neil moved the conversation tactfully away from that theme. 'Let's see, my rental agreement expires at the end of October. So I'll come to Sydney then. Easy peasy.'

'Just in time for spring,' said Alice.

Neil slid his arms around her. 'I don't care what time of the year it is,' he said. 'And anyway, by then my credit card will have recovered. It's a bit maxed out now.' He felt the ring on her finger.

Alice pulled away from him, and she saw he was grinning. It dawned on her that they hadn't yet delved into the practicalities. Like money. 'You do have enough… I mean, you can afford the airfare?' she said anxiously.

'Sure. I was only messing with you. I'll have my car to sell, for

160

one thing. And also, when my mom died a few years ago she left my brother and me quite a tidy sum between us, from the sale of her house. I haven't touched that yet.'

'Same here. Mum left her money to me, and a lot of that was from her house sale. The will is still going through probate, but the rest of the process can get sorted out remotely. Because I won't have a job after the end of the year, that financial safety net will take a lot of the pressure off.'

'So,' said Neil, lightly, 'in a few months' time we'll be a couple of fit, healthy, unemployed people with a bit of cash to jingle in our pockets. We should do something.'

Alice looked at him. 'Are you serious?'

Neil stopped grinning and met her look with the same gravity 'I am now,' he said.

*

The next morning, Alice's final morning, she lay quietly in bed next to Neil, aware of his breathing and slight stirrings. She silently picked up her phone from where it lay on the bedside table and checked the time: nearly six o'clock. She hadn't slept at all well, but that was hardly surprising given everything that had happened in the last day. First, the wonderful decision that Neil was going to come to Australia, then on top of it all – this new, crazy idea.

They had sat cross-legged on the floor facing each other and cautiously unpacked this nascent idea that they should 'do something'.

Neil started them off. 'I've never been to Australia. We could do a sort of long holiday, and you could show me all the sights.'

'A good plan if I may say so except for one thing. I've never been out of New South Wales.'

'Then a trip round Australia would be an adventure for us both. And you wouldn't have to be too far away from your family.'

Alice nodded thoughtfully. 'I see what you're saying. But if you're one thousand or five thousand miles from your home it doesn't really matter. It's just a few more hours on a plane and you can still keep in touch online, like I'm doing now.' She felt a delicious, exhilarating wantonness bubbling up inside her. 'If we really want an adventure, we could go backpacking to another country altogether.'

'Wow. Who is this woman with all these audacious ideas?'

'I'm not usually reckless like this. It must be you; you've released the hidden explorer in me. I never even went on a gap year or anything after university.'

'Me neither. Well, now's our chance, I guess. Where have you got in mind?'

'Oh, I really don't know.' She spread her arms wide. 'The world's our oyster, whatever that means.'

Neil gave her a slightly bemused, alarmed look, as if he had unleased something he thought he was familiar with but was now not so sure. 'I haven't been to the Far East at all. So somewhere there would work for me. Malaysia? Is that even in the Far East?'

'It certainly is. Or what about Indonesia, with all those islands?'

'Or Singapore? Or Hong Kong?' said Neil.

'Or China?' said Alice.

'China? Have you seen me with chopsticks?'

They both fell about laughing as they thought of more and more outrageous places that they could go to, some of which they weren't sure were real. Their laughter was acquiring a slightly hysterical edge, and Alice realised what was happening. She was desperately pushing away the knowledge that very soon she would be on the plane leaving Neil behind. She calmed down and became solemn then. 'After tomorrow I'm not going to see you for a few weeks,' she said.

'That's true. But it's only the ending of this phase of our being together. We've got other beginnings. And we've got plenty of time to discuss the future. We will be in touch every day, won't we?' said Neil.

'You bet!' said Alice.

Neil took her hand. 'Come on. Let's go to bed.'

*

The next morning Alice checked her passport and boarding pass yet again. She also checked her watch; it wasn't time to go yet. She caught Neil covertly looking at the time too. Nothing about them was normal or easy this morning. They were polite to each other, but the easy banter was now of another time.

'We might as well sit down with our coffee,' said Neil, and they perched on their chairs at the kitchen table, sipping awkwardly.

'There's something I keep thinking about,' said Alice. Neil waited for her to continue. She frowned and stared into her coffee mug. 'The ring. The ring that has caused so much trouble. We know now that it was a fake, and Mr Branson the jeweller said that the stones had not been replaced. So it never did have diamonds in it. What I'm wondering is, did Mum know that? Did Dad know? Did anybody know before that?' She looked up in puzzlement at Neil.

Neil thought for a moment. 'What you told me was that the family folklore, as handed down, said that one of your ancestors stole the ring from a gypsy who was peddling their wares, right?' When Alice agreed he said, 'It seems to me pretty unlikely that a gypsy would have something like a diamond ring in their tray. I said that to you when you first told me the story.'

Alice nodded in agreement. 'So I wonder when the lie first started? Did my great-great grandfather or whatever he was, know or guess that it wasn't real diamonds but used it anyway to woo his sweetheart?'

'Who knows? It's lost in the mists of time. A pretty romantic story anyway, you've got to admit.'

'It certainly is.' Alice pondered. 'Do you know, from the way Mum talked about the ring, I'm fairly sure she truly believed it was diamonds. There was her wish to give to me when I got married, for instance. And I wouldn't take it.' Alice felt a dim pang of regret at the memory.

'It's all in the past now, Alice.'

'Yes, it's in the past,' Alice held her hand out and inspected it. 'But this ring isn't in the past. Look how it sparkles! I absolutely

163

love it, you know that don't you, Neil? I think that other ring is cursed.'

'Cursed? You don't really believe in such things, do you?'

'Well, it didn't exactly bring good luck to you and me.'

It was too early for Alice to leave for the airport yet, so they just sat at the breakfast table quietly munching toast.

'You're staring at me,' said Neil. 'What? Have I got jam on my face or something?' He wiped his mouth with his fingers.

'No,' said Alice. 'I'm trying to capture your image right now. Every nuance.'

Neil softened his expression. 'You'll be seeing me every day on screen. And we said we're not going to be sad when you go, remember?'

'You're right,' said Alice. 'And anyway, I've decided there's something I need to do.' She pushed her plate away decisively and stood up. 'Will you come with me to the garden, please?'

They went out through the French doors. The weather was overcast but not raining. They passed the bench and went beyond the patio to the where the edge of the garden was quite overgrown. Pushing their way through some low bushes they came to the chain link fence that marked the edge of the property. Just beyond the fence was the little river, a tributary of the larger one that flowed through the town. The river trickled its way pleasantly over the stones and rocks.

'Why are we here?' said Neil.

'I think you can probably guess,' said Alice. Out of her pocket she drew the ring and placed it on her palm. Now, to her, its very presence seemed truly malevolent. 'This ring has caused nothing but trouble. I want to be rid of it, once and for all. So here goes.' She hurled the ring towards the river. For one split second she thought her aim had been poor, because it bounced onto a rock, but it ricocheted off and was swallowed by the water.

*

It was Christmas Day. I thought I was finished with festivities like this on the beach, thought Alice, but here I am again. Mum would be pleased, if she could see us. Alice allowed herself to imagine that Mum was in fact watching them in her benign way. She would see the beach, as crowded as ever because it was Christmas Day, with all the folks enjoying the Sydney sunshine and summer temperatures. She would see Alice and Zoe setting up the chairs and the barbeque and setting out various snacks. Then she would see Neil and Joe trudging over the warm sand with a cool box each that housed the drink and the meats. They were laughing and chatting idly. Alice could feel Mum's approval.

'This sure beats a freezing day in New York for a Christmas celebration,' said Neil. He pulled out cold beers for everyone from the cool box. Joe busied himself getting out the steaks and the rolls.

When they all had a bottle in their hand, Alice cleared her throat theatrically and said, 'I'd like to propose a toast and say a few words'. Both the kids groaned and rolled their eyes, which Alice ignored. 'I'd like to ask us all to remember a special lady, that's Mum, Granny, Lucy, whatever you call her. She would have loved to be with us today, but it wasn't to be.' They all drank, and Zoe and Joe looked slightly uncomfortable. 'And,' continued Alice, 'Zoe and Joe, I want to thank you for being so welcoming to Neil. For welcoming him to Sydney and to my home. You've been great.'

After another round of swigging Zoe said, 'I think it's awesome that you two are going travelling soon. All my friends think I've got the coolest mom ever.'

'I'm glad your mom talked me into it,' said Neil, sliding his arm round Alice and giving her a big sloppy kiss.

'Yuk,' said Joe, and busied himself with putting steaks on the barbeque and spearing a split roll with the toasting fork.